CONTENTS

BEJEWELLED CROWN

'Kalki' is the pen name of Ramaswamy Krishnamurthy (1899–1954), whose career in writing and journalism began as activism during the struggle for Indian independence. He served as editor of the popular Tamil magazine *Ananda Vikatan* before launching *Kalki*. The magazine—and eventually its founder—was named for the mythological tenth avatar of Vishnu to symbolise a vision to 'destroy regressive regimes, express radical thoughts, take readers into new directions, and create a new era'. Kalki wrote several novels, including *Parthiban Kanavu* and *Sivakamiyin Sabadam*, as well as political essays, film reviews, dance and music critiques, and scholarly work.

Nandini Krishnan is the author of *Hitched: The Modern Woman and Arranged Marriage* and *Invisible Men: Inside India's Transmasculine Networks*. She has translated two of Perumal Murugan's works into English: *Estuary* and *Four Strokes of Luck*. She was shortlisted for the PEN Presents translation prize 2022 and the Ali Jawad Zaidi Memorial Prize for translation from Urdu 2022. She is an alumna of the Writer's Bloc playwrights' workshop by the Royal Court Theatre, London. Her novel-in-manuscript was a winner of the Caravan Writers of India Festival contest and showcased at the Writers of the World Festival, Paris, 2014.

PONNIYIN SELVAN BOOK 7

BEJEWELLED CROWN

KALKI

TRANSLATED BY
NANDINI KRISHNAN

ekadā

ekadā

First published in Tamil as *Ponniyin Selvan*

Published in English in 2026 by Ekadā, an imprint of Westland Books, a division of Nasadiya Technologies Private Limited

No. 269/2B, First Floor, 'Irai Arul', Vimalraj Street, Nethaji Nagar, Alapakkam Main Road, Maduravoyal, Chennai 600095

Westland, the Westland logo, Ekadā and the Ekadā logo are the trademarks of Nasadiya Technologies Private Limited, or its affiliates.

ISBN: 9789371977494

10 9 8 7 6 5 4 3 2 1

This is a work of fiction. Names, characters, organisations, places, events and incidents are either products of the author's imagination or used fictitiously.

Typeset by Jojy Philip

Printed at Parksons Graphics Pvt. Ltd

1

BY THE BANKS OF THE KEDILAM

The Kedilam[1] is one of the rivers whose waters irrigate the lands of Tirumunaippadi. This lush setting also has a special place in history. Tiruvadigai Veerattaanam, where Lord Shiva cured Appar[2], is on the banks of this river[3], and not far off is Tirunavalur, where the same god appeared before Sundaramurti[4].

The spot where the Rajpath crossed the Kedilam was always abuzz with the chirping of birds and the flapping of their wings. Travellers typically rested here, and allowed their horses and cows to graze while they themselves ate. Crows waited for scraps from the travellers' food. Young men would throw grains in the air to see birds fight over them in flight.

It was the beginning of the month of Aippasi, and the flow of water was more rapid than usual. This excited the sojourners, who frolicked in the river after stopping for lunch.

That day, a loud noise from nearby drowned out the voices of people, animals and birds alike. Some of the surprised travellers waded back to shore to see what its source might be.

At first, all they could see was a cloud of dust. Then, they could make out the silhouettes of elephants, horses, palanquins and eventually soldiers who appeared to be escorting a royal.

Soon enough, the drummers and criers appeared.

Pannirandaam praayaththil porkkalam pugunda veeradiveerar
Veerapandiyan thalaikkonda koparakesari
Irattai mandalaththaar soppanaththil kandu anjum singham
Thondai mandaladipati, vadadisai mahatanda nayagar
Moondru ulagamudaya Sundara Chozha Chakravartiyin tirumaganaar
Aditya Karikala Chozha Maharaja varugiraar! Paraak!

Intrepid warrior who went out to battle when he was all of twelve,
The lion of the royal clan, who beheaded Veerapandiyan
And haunts the nightmares of soldiers from Irattai Mandalam
The leader of Thondai Mandalam, Mahatanda Nayagar of the Northern Front
The son of Sundara Chozha Chakravarti who rules the three worlds
Aditya Karikala Chozha Maharaja is here! Paraak!

The very earth echoed with these stentorian cries, and everyone by the Kedilam river rushed to either side of the Rajpath for a glimpse of this storied hero.

The drummers, trumpeters and bearers of cymbals were the first to arrive with the criers. Next came three horses in the distance. The riders were all young men.

The people lining the street jostled each other as they tried to identify them.

'The one in the middle is Aditya Karikalar! Can't you tell from his crown! Oh, how it dazzles in the sunlight!'

'That is just an ordinary crown! Imagine how he will look when he dons the bejewelled crown of Karikaal Valavan! That would shine like a million suns!'

'That is not the crown of Karikaal Valavan, thambi! That is simply a legend. The crown Sundara Chozhar wears was forged in Parantaka Chakravarti's time. That is the crown that Aditya Karikalar will wear. Who knows for how long Sundara Chozhar will continue to wear it!'

'People have been saying this for some time, that Sundara Chozhar is not long for this world. But he's still here. He will be a Chiranjeevi[5], I think!'

'If only! For as long as he is alive, the land won't erupt in confusion and conflict!'

'One can never tell. Ever since news came of Ponniyin Selvan drowning at sea, Chozha Naadu has turned into a sea of confusion! Who knows when the conflict will begin?'

'Conflict between whom? And over what?'

'Between the Pazhuvettaraiyar and Kodumbalur clans, I believe. The suzerain kings have gathered at Kadambur Sambuvarayar's palace for a conference to resolve the issue without conflict, apparently. That is where Aditya Karikalar is headed too!'

'The horses are almost here! Don't talk so loudly!' a man hissed. 'Do you see how wan Aditya Karikalar looks?'

'What did you expect? He would give his life for his brother, and now there are rumours that the brother is dead! There is no news confirming anything. Aditya Karikalar must be tearing his hair out with anxiety! And their father is bedridden too.'

'His father has been ailing for a long time. And when a prince goes to war, one is prepared for anything to happen. So, those are not the reasons for Aditya Karikalar's gloom. He wants to march on Irattai Mandalam. And he is upset that that has not come to pass!'

'Whyever not? Who is stopping him?'

'Who else? The Pazhuvettaraiyar brothers! They have refused to give him the financial and logistical support he needs.'

'You people are coming up with all sorts of moronic ideas, all imagined! None of you knows the real reason for his sorrow!' one man said.

'O omniscient lord! Enlighten us, why don't you?' another said.

'Aditya Karikalar was in love with some girl from Pandiya Naadu. When the prince had gone to war in Vadapennai, Periya Pazhuvettaraiyar went and married that girl. It is she who is now the Pazhuvoor Ilaiya Rani, omnipotent in Chozha Naadu. Aditya Karikalar has been miserable ever since he heard of this.'

'Perhaps, perhaps! Our elders have said that it is women who cause world wars!'

'Which elders, thambi? I've never heard of anything more insane! Why would a girl whom the prince desires choose a doddering old man over him? It is foolish enough to say it, and even more foolish to believe it!'

'Oh, really? Then why is Aditya Karikalar still unmarried? Would you like to come up with a sane explanation for that, then?'

'Be quiet now! They can practically hear us! The man on the prince's right is Parthibendra Pallavan, it seems. Who is on his left? Vandiyadevan of the Vaanar clan?'

'No, no. It is Kadambur Sambuvarayar's son Kandamaaran. Sambuvarayar was worried the prince might not be moved by an olai, and so he sent his son to personally invite him to the palace.'

'So, clearly, it is a matter of great importance.'

'Yes, it could have to do with royal matters. Or it could have to do with nuptial matters too. The suzerain kings have all been vying for his hand, for their daughters. His first wife will be the one who sits by his side on the Chozha throne, won't she?'

As the subjects gossiped away, the three horses stopped by the river bank. Some way behind them, a chariot came to a halt under a peepul tree. The occupant of the chariot was Tirukkovalur Malayaman, well into his eighties.

Aditya Karikalan, sitting on his horse, turned to look at his grandfather.

2

GRANDFATHER AND GRANDSON

The old man in the chariot gestured to Aditya Karikalan, who approached him on his horse.

'Kuzhandaai[1]! Karikala! I'm planning to take leave of you all here and return to Tirukkovalur. Before I go, I have some important things to tell you. Get off your horse now and accompany me to the peepul tree, where we can sit, won't you?'

'As you wish, thatha!' Aditya Karikalan said, jumping off his horse.

As grandfather and grandson made their way to the tree, Parthibendran turned to Kandamaaran and said, 'What a relief! I was afraid the old man would accompany us all the way.'

'I was planning to drown him in the Vellaaru if he stuck around much longer,' Kandamaaran said, and the two laughed.

In the meantime, Tirukkovalur Malayaman was looking at his grandson.

'Aditya,' he said at last, 'today marks twenty-four years since you were born. It was in my palace in Tirukkovalur that you were born! I remember the celebrations as if they ended just yesterday. The people of your clan, my relatives and suzerain kings from Chozha Naadu and Thondai Naadu were all there. The soldiers who escorted them numbered over thirty thousand! Oh, the festivities! Not even your father's coronation was as grand a ceremony, my child! In those three days, I emptied hundred years' worth of ancestral wealth from my treasury!

'Your great-grandfather Parantaka Chakravarti himself came to Tirukkovalur at the time. Your great-uncle Kandaradityar and your father Sundara Chozhar were there too. When they learnt that the baby was a boy, their joy knew no bounds. An heir had been born, a prince who would carry on the line and make this dynasty's story ever more glorious. Your grandfather's elder brothers had no offspring, and your father was Arinjayan's sole heir. When he was your age, he was the very epitome of pulchritude. No one had ever seen such a good-looking man in Chozha Naadu, or any other Tamil land for that matter. This caused some trouble for your father. Everyone adored him. The women of the royal palace used to dress him up as a girl during his infancy and childhood, and sigh about how wonderful it would have been if he had been born a woman. Every king from Lanka to the Vindhyas practically begged for his hand in marriage to their daughters. Not only was he the equal of Arjuna and Manmadha where looks were concerned but he was also heir to the Chozha throne. In the end, I was the one who had the honour of becoming his father-in-law.

'Our clan has never set much store by physical beauty, perhaps because we have never possessed it. We measure the beauty of men by the number of scars from war wounds on their bodies. As for the women, it is their chastity and demeanour which make them beautiful. When my daughter was chosen to be your father's wife, all of Malayamanaadu erupted in joy. And all the suzerain kings were mad with envy. It didn't bother me. Your parents' wedding in Thanjai was so grand that all three worlds came to a standstill to gawk at the celebrations. Even so, they were as nothing compared to the festivities in Tirukkovalur at your birth. There were long debates over the name you should be given. Some people said you must be named after Karikaal Valavan, while others including myself felt you should be named after your great-uncle and the greatest war hero we had seen, Rajadityar. In the end, it was decided you should have a combination of those two names, "Aditya Karikalan".

'Look there, Aditya! Do you see the top of the temple gopuram of Tirunavalur? That was the place of birth of Nambi Aroorar Sundarmurti. Twenty-five years ago, your great-uncle Rajadityar had set up camp there. I've read of great warriors in stories and epics, and I have seen great warriors in my own lifetime. But

I have never seen or heard of a hero like Rajadityar. Anyone who has seen him on the battlefield will tell you the same.

'He was preparing to march on the northern lands. He was gathering a grand army here. He was determined to lay siege to the fort of Kannara Devan, the king of Irattai Mandalam and capture his capital city Manyakheta[2]. He intended to destroy the city as the Pallava emperor Mamalla Chakravarti had destroyed Vatapi. He felt the pride of the Irattai Mandalam dynasty could only be felled by burning the capital. And this would give him the name and fame that Mamallar had won. Was it an easy task to gather an army large enough to achieve this? They say it took Mamallar seven years to gather his army. Rajadityar said he didn't need as much time, three or four years would be enough. He chose the land between the Kedilam and Thenpennai rivers as the place where he would gather and train these warriors.

'Aditya! If only you could have seen this place at the time! Every man who has seen it will remember it to his dying day. Rajadityar stayed in Tirunavalur with thirty thousand soldiers. The Chera Naadu suzerain king Vellan Kumaran had camped with twenty thousand warriors at Mudiyur, by the banks of the Pennai river. Your grandfather Arinjayan was in Tirukkovalur with me, and together we got fifty thousand soldiers for the war effort. Kodumbalur Periya Velaan, and the man who is now the curse of Chozha Naadu, Periya

Pazhuvettaraiyar, camped between these two rivers, along with Kadambur Sambuvarayan, Munaiyatharayan who was the king of Tirumunaippadi, Mazhanaattu Mazhuvarayan, Kunrathoor Kizhaan, Vaidumbarayan and several others. Each had brought his army along. Elephants, horses, infantry ... they were all there. We would have mock battles between the armies to train for war. You should have felt the earth tremble as elephants clashed in these mock battles! And when the horses flew by, bearing soldiers whose spears glinted in the sun it was as if the sea was rising to drown the earth! As soldiers practised archery, the very firmament would disappear behind the arrows. When thousands of soldiers roared as one, "Naavalo Naaval!" and attacked their "enemies", you would think it was the end of the world. People came in hordes to watch us train.

'The people of Tirumunaippadi Naadu and Nadu Naadu are not just good-hearted, they are also truly courageous. Our setting up camp here was disastrous to the cultivation of their crops. But they didn't care. And it was to thank them that Rajadityar raised several dams to irrigate these lands. He had the waters diverted from Kollidam and brought to the Veeranarayanapuram lake. Aditya, it is Kadambur Sambuvarayan who has benefited most from that dam. I'm not able to reconcile the man who fell at Rajadityar's feet that day with this influential, wealthy person he has become now.'

Aditya Karikalan interrupted him to say, 'Thatha! Why do you care about Sambuvarayar's wealth and influence? Tell me about the war at Takkolam. When did that grand army leave from here? And why was it that, in spite of such thorough preparation and my great-uncle's brilliance and bravery on the battlefield, our armies lost? You were on that battlefield, weren't you? You must have seen it all unfold!'

'Yes, I was and yes, I did. I was coming to that when you asked. Rajadityar was preparing the various regiments—elephantry, cavalry, infantry, chariots—to wage war in far-off lands that he intended to conquer one after the other. For various reasons, he wasn't able to leave at the time he wanted to. Then news came of war having restarted in Lanka. Some of the armies had to be diverted to deal with that. The emperor did not want the remaining armies to march to the north while the war was on so far down south, in case backup was needed. Rajadityar was not able to counter his father's wishes. He waited patiently for the war in Lanka to end. But the enemies did not wait. Kannara Devan got together a large army to march on Chozha Naadu, and began to journey southwards. The Ganga king Butuga joined him with his own large army. When the two armies met, it was as if two seas had churned together to form an ocean. The thousands of war elephants were as whales in that ocean and the tens of thousands of horses as crocodilefish. They say that at the time of Pralayam[3], the seven seas will drown all land. When these armies came down to the south, it was as if they were the seven seas rising to drown us. That was what our spies, who flew like the wind to warn us of the approaching danger, told us.

'However, Parantaka Chakravarti said this was just as well. It was a better tactic to draw the enemy to us and then surround them than to exhaust our soldiers by making them go on a long march to strange lands with whose vagaries they were unfamiliar. It was only after the enemy had reached Vadavengadam that the emperor gave us the go-ahead to march forward.

'Rajadityar had already left, without waiting for permission. The infantry numbered three hundred thousand, the cavalry fifty thousand, the elephantry ten thousand and the chariots two thousand. There were three hundred and twenty generals heading the armies of thirty-two suzerain kings. I had the good fortune to count myself among them. And the ill fortune of returning alive.

'After a march of three days, our armies met those of the enemy at Takkolam, two kaadhams to the north of Kanchi.

'Aditya! We have heard of the epic battles of yore, Indra and Vritra, Rama and Ravana, the Pandavas and Kauravas. But those who have witnessed the battle of Takkolam will aver that those epic wars were as nothing in comparison to what they saw. The enemy's army was nearly twofold the strength of ours. Apparently, there were five hundred thousand soldiers and thirty thousand war elephants. So what? They did not have Rajadityar for their senapati. And so Veeralakshmi and Jayalakshmi decided to go with us.

'The war went on for ten days. It was impossible to count the bodies on either side. Dead elephants lay like dark mountains. Even so, it was the enemy that suffered the greater losses. They soon realised why. Everywhere Rajadityar's elephant went, Jayalakshmi followed. The goddess of victory had chosen her side. And your great-uncle found his way to whichever part of the battlefield needed his help, wherever the soldiers were tiring. The moment they saw the elephant and the peerless warrior seated on the howdah, our soldiers found a new lease of life. Their exhaustion overcome, they attacked their enemies with twice, even thrice, the strength. Having observed this for ten days, the enemy came up with a callous conspiracy. It was only later that we realised it was a conspiracy. It was Butuga who came up with this plan and executed it.

'That evil man mounted his elephant bearing a flag of peace, and raised both hands in the air, calling "Sharanam! Sharanam!" to signify his surrender. Rajadityar was at the spot. Butuga must have recognised him from the tiger flag his elephant bore. When the intrepid Rajadityar saw an enemy surrendering, his heart melted. He was willing to end the war. He wanted to know whether both Kannara Devan and Butuga were begging for an end to hostilities or whether it was Butuga alone. And so, he blew his conch and asked his bodyguards to move away. He gestured to Butuga to approach. Butuga had folded his hands in deference and remained that way until he got close to Rajadityar, close enough for your great-uncle to see that he was sobbing from despair. At this, your great-uncle felt even sorrier for him.

'At the time, Rajadityar did not remember the words of Tamizhagam's great poet, Tiruvalluvar:

Thozhukai ullum padaiyodungum onnaar
Azhudakan neerum anaiththu

Pleading hands may well hide enemy knives
Their prayers false as the tears of foes.

'The tears of this foe softened Rajadityar's heart and he allowed him to come even closer. He asked Butuga, "What news do you bring?" Butuga's response enraged him. Butuga said it had become evident that he and Kannara Devan would be defeated, and when he had approached Kannara Devan suggesting surrender, the latter had refused, leaving him with no choice but to switch allegiances. Rajadityar was so disgusted he let loose a volley of insults, saying there was no place by his side for such an unprincipled man. Even as he was telling him to return and face war, for he was rejecting the surrender, Butuga did that awful thing within the blink of an eye. He reached for the bow and quiver he had hidden away, strung the bow and shot the arrow at close range. It was a poisoned arrow and struck

Rajadityar right in the chest. He fell backwards. None of us had expected this, and none of us even realised what had happened. Even those standing nearby had only heard Rajadityar shout to Butuga to go back to war, and didn't understand what it meant even as the Ganga king spurred his elephant on and fled.

'When the news of Rajadityar's death spread, it was as if the life had gone out of every single one of our soldiers. In their grief, they forgot that they were on the battlefield. The suzerain kings and generals and soldiers all sank as one, lamenting instead of fighting, mourning instead of waging war. Soon, our armies had to retreat as the sea surged at us. The sea of two armies, the sea of two cheats. They hunted us down as we ran. I was among those who turned and ran, Aditya! They chased us down, right up to this river, the Kedilam River. It was here that we came to our senses. It was on our training ground that we remembered who we were, that we fought back. We halted their march. I went to Tirukkovalur and took my family to Malai Naadu to the west. I gathered armies right there and came back here. We attacked the enemy, but it took us years to beat them back. Even so, they occupied pockets here and gave us trouble. Kanchi was in their hands until three years ago, when you marched here after defeating Veerapandiyan and claimed it back …'

Aditya Karikalan interrupted his grandfather again now. 'Thatha!' he said. 'I've heard this story many times before. But I could never, ever tire of hearing the tale of the Takkolam war and the feats of Rajadityar in that war. Why did you bring this up now, though?'

'Kuzhandaai! Your great-uncle's dream was to expand the Chozha empire so it stretched from Lanka to Ganga. He lost his life before that dream came true. Everyone says my grandson Aditya Karikalan is as great a warrior as Rajadityar. The people of Tamizhagam believe it is you who will fulfil his unrealised dreams. But you must not fall for a trick as he did; you must not allow yourself to be betrayed as he did. That is why I'm reminding you of what happened to him.'

'Thatha! My great-uncle lost his life on the battlefield, to the conspiracy of enemies. But how is that relevant to me? I'm not headed to battle. And I'm not going to meet enemies who will trap me either. I'm going to meet my father's dearest friends, aren't I? Why would they conspire against me or trap me in any way?'

'Listen, Karikala! The very same poet who said 'pleading hands could hide enemy knives and that their prayers are as false as their tears' has also said:

Vaalpol pagaivarai anjarka anjuga
Kelpol pagaivar thodarbu

Fear not the enemy who is overt as a sword; fear, rather
The covert enemy pledging troth and friendship.

'Kuzhandaai! You will be among enemies posing as friends. You insisted on going despite my saying you shouldn't. They claim they're inviting you to discuss a dispute over governance. I also hear that they plan to foist one of Sambuvarayan's daughters on you. But I don't know what their real motive is. You cannot know either. There are kings lining up to give you their daughters, even kings from far-off lands. Why do you want to have anything to do with Sambuvarayan's daughter? I also hear that they are bringing you a proposal to divide the empire into two, one to be ruled by you and another by Madurantakan. I don't know what conspiracy or plot awaits you there. Whatever the case may be, I'm going to Tirukkovalur now to gather my armies and bring them to the banks of the Vellaru. If you should have any cause for suspicion during your stay at Sambuvarayan's palace, send word to me right away! And ...'

Malayaman paused suddenly, realising that Aditya Karikalan was distracted by something else and was no longer paying him attention.

'Thatha! Look there!' Aditya Karikalan said in a choked voice.

The old man squinted anxiously in the direction towards which his grandson was pointing, trying to see what the prince had seen.

3

THE EAGLE AND THE DOVE

Aditya Karikalan was pointing at one of the mandapams by the seaside. The stone structure must have been constructed by an altruist who wanted to provide travellers with some shelter from the sun and the rain. Having borne the brunt of the weather's vagaries, the stone was rather worse for the wear, but one could still see the sculptures that had been carved into it. Malayaman's fading eyesight, however, did not allow him to see their features clearly.

'Do you see, thatha?' Aditya Karikalan asked.

'Kuzhandaai! You're referring to that mandapam, aren't you? I don't see anything else. The mandapam is empty too. I don't see anyone inside,' he said.

'Thatha! It is only now that it strikes me that you've got old. Your eyesight is not what it used to be. Look there! Do you see that huge Rajali eagle? What an enormous bird it is! Look at its wingspan! Terrible, terrible! How cruel it is! It has a tiny dove in its claws, do you see? Its sharp talons have dug into the flesh of that dove, don't you see? Kadavule, what is this! What a wonder! Another little dove has come there, thatha! It is circling around that gigantic Rajali! It's pleading with the eagle! The dove the Rajali has caught must be this dove's lover! She's begging the eagle for mercy, asking him to spare her lover's life! Thatha! Is the dove pleading or fighting? The way she's flapping her wings, it is as if she's readying for battle! Kadavule! How brave that girl is! A little dove taking on the Rajali, for the sake of her lover! She's going to fight with that rakshasha of a bird! Thatha! Do you think that Rajali will relent? No, no, never! It has killed so many, many doves like this! That cursed Rajali! Oh, you terrible, horrible bird! Here, *I'm* going to kill you!'

And with that Aditya Karikalan reached for a heavy rock lying nearby and hurled it at the mandapam. The rock hit the wall and fell into a corner.

'Rakshasha!' Aditya Karikalan shouted. 'You deserved that!'

And he began to laugh.

The old man had already been worrying about his grandson's sanity. Now, he grew more concerned.

'Thatha! Why are you staring at me like that? Go closer to the mandapam and you'll see,' Aditya Karikalan said.

Malayaman did as he said, and stared at the point where the rock Karikalan had hurled now lay. He could see a sculpture there. It did depict a Rajali eagle carrying a dove in its talons, while another dove was seen in flight as if readying for battle with the Rajali.

Malayaman returned to the spot where his grandson was sitting and said, 'Kuzhandaai! It *is* true that I've grown old! My eyesight has lost its sharpness. It was only after I got close that I could see the carving. The sculptor's work is good.'

'The sculptor's work is good? It's an artistic marvel, thatha! The virtuoso who crafted this must have been a sculptor from the era of Mahendravarmar Mamallar! When I first saw it, it was as if it was happening before my very eyes, as if it was real!'

'Aditya! It is not just the stonework that is a marvel, but your eyesight. And your mind. How many travellers go this way. Most of them would not even have noticed that stunning carving. The few who do would just see it as part of the landscape. It is a very, very select group that would gaze upon it as you do and be as awed as you are.'

'I'm not awed, thatha! I'm angry. I'm enraged! I want to break that sculpture right now. I don't even feel like praising the man who conjured such an awful image.'

'Karikala! What is this bizarre change that has come over you? When did your warrior's heart begin to bleed like this? It is in the very nature of the Rajali to kill the dove. If a lion were to pity a goat, it cannot be a lion any longer. It would turn into a goat, in spirit, if nothing else. Those who wish to sit on a throne must be ready to kill enemies and traitors. A king who desires to conquer the entire world must kill other kings! How can a Rajali be a Rajali if it were to desist from killing doves? Why does this sculpture trouble you so much?'

'Thatha! I can't fault anything you've said. But shouldn't the Rajali feel pity for that female dove? Shouldn't he be moved by her love for the male dove and release him? Aiya, tell me yourself … let's say you're about to kill your enemy, when his lover comes up to you and falls at your feet, begging you to spare his life. What would you do? Wouldn't your heart feel pity for her?'

'If a woman did as you say, I would kick her away with one foot and kill my enemy before her eyes, Karikala. There is no doubt about it. Valluvar has said praying hands can hold preying swords, that the words of enemies are as false as their tears. Women's tears are even more dangerous than those of men, because women's tears have the power to make men melt. A man who allows himself to melt can never achieve great things. Why, he would be even lowlier than a woman!'

'Thatha! What is this? Why do you speak in such a degrading manner about women? Don't you see that you're insulting my mother too when you speak of her sex this way?'

'Kuzhandaai! Hear my words carefully. My love for your mother knows no bounds. I had six sons, sons who were the equal of Bhima and Arjuna in battle. And I lost all of them to war. Not even the news of their deaths pained me as much as the moment when I gave your mother away in marriage. I knew she would sit on the Chozha throne, and yet I was beside myself with grief at being separated from my beloved child. But did I let anyone see that sorrow? Did I even tell her my feelings? Of course not! On the eve of her wedding, do you know what I told her? "My daughter! You're about to marry a man who will conquer the entire world. But let that not make you arrogant! Marrying a man of such fame and fortitude will only bring you sorrow. Truth be told, many of the palace servants who wait on you will be happier than you. Prepare yourself for sorrow and anxiety and grief. If you don't have children, your husband will certainly marry other women. But let that not trouble you. If you do have children, raise them to become heroes. And if you hear that they have died in battle, you must not shed a single tear. When your husband is happy, rejoice with him. When he is sad, try to cheer him up! If he were to fall ill, stay by his side and attend to his every need. If he were to die, burn in his pyre with him![1] Your heart may bleed, but your eyes must remain dry! This is the nature of women from the Malayaman clan, and you must live up to this reputation!" I said to her. And your mother has followed every single bit of advice and instruction I gave her. Karikala! She has raised you and your brother to become peerless warriors. She stays by your ailing father's side night and day. Every time I think of my daughter, my shoulders grow wider and broader with pride!'

'Thatha, my pride knows no bounds when I think of my mother. But let me ask you something. If some terrible enemy were to approach my father, my ailing father, dagger in hand … what would my mother do? Wouldn't she sob and beg him to spare her husband's life? Most important, let's say this enemy was someone my mother already knew …'

'Kuzhandaai! Your mother would never beg an enemy to spare her husband's life. Malayaman's daughter would never let the clan of her birth and the clan into which she married down that way! What humiliation! No, she would never do that. She would see her husband's enemy as her own enemy, and she would never bow down to an enemy or sob to him or beg for mercy. If her husband were to be killed, she would throw herself upon his body and die with him. Or, she would harden her heart and live on without him until she avenged his death.'

Aditya Karikalan heard him out and heaved a heavy sigh 'All right, thatha, shall I take your leave?'

'Must you absolutely go?'

'Why do you still have doubts, thatha! We're more than halfway to our destination!'

'Yes, we are. I asked you not to go at first. And then, I said you should. When we got the news about your brother, it seemed a good idea for you to go there and … well, I don't believe Arulmozhi Varman is dead.'

'I don't either.'

'In your father's youth, he went missing for some time. Your brother too must be alive, on one of those islands. He will return soon. However, I know most of the empire does not share this belief. The news of his death has created a furore. Your parents must be devastated. It is important that you be by their side at this time, to console them and reassure them. And it is better that you go as a friend than an enemy of the Pazhuvettaraiyar brothers. That is why I eventually acquiesced in your accepting Sambuvarayar's invitation. It was on purpose that he did not invite me. If he had, I'd have accompanied you.'

'Thatha! Why are you so scared for me? Do you think I'm that helpless?' Karikalan asked.

'No, thambi, no! Don't I know how superlative a warrior you are? I would send you out alone to face ten thousand armed enemy soldiers! But I hesitate to send you alone to a woman whose tears can melt your heart.'

'I haven't heard anything that would make me think Sambuvarayar's daughter is the kind who manipulates men. I believe she hesitates to so much as meet strangers! Kandamaaran has told me. And I'm not going to hurry into a marriage without my parents' opinion. I'm also aware that two of the women born into your own clan are as yet unmarried …'

'Aditya, I'm not thinking along those lines at all. Yes, two of my eldest son's daughters are of marriageable age, but I don't have any plans of foisting either on you. The suzerain kings are jealous enough of me already. Why give them further cause? I'd much rather you marry Sambuvarayar's daughter. I've become old now, my body is weak … and sometimes, my heart becomes weak too. I worry that I will not see my beloved grandson again. What if this is the last time I see you? I'm of no use to you anymore. You need new friends, people you can trust, people who care for you and who will look out for you, who are interested in your well-being. And so, if you decide to marry Sambuvarayar's daughter, I would be quite happy.'

'Thatha! I wouldn't do such a thing even for your happiness. I've accepted Sambuvarayar's invitation neither in the interest of forging a friendship with him nor in the interest of forging an alliance with his daughter. You can set your mind at rest on that account.'

'Then why have you accepted his invitation, my child? Can't you tell me the truth? I happened to hear some of the exchanges between your two friends. I believe that Mohini Pisaasu whom Periya Pazhuvettaraiyan married after he had crossed sixty has sent you an olai? They say that was the reason you accepted the invitation. Is that true?'

'Yes, thatha, it is,' Aditya Karikalan said.

'Kadavule! How can such a thing come to pass? Karikala, listen to me carefully. The Chozha dynasty into which you were born is two millennia old. Some of your ancestors have ruled the entire world. At other times, your clan has been reduced to ruling only Uraiyur and the territories around it. There are those who followed Lord Rama's footsteps in taking no more than one wife. And there are others who married tens of women and had an army of children. Some were devotees of Shiva, some were devotees of Vishnu and some were non-believers. But not one of them was short on ethics. None has desired another man's wife. Kuzhandaai! Marry as many women as you want, women who have not known another man's touch. Your great-grandfather Parantaka Chakravarti had seven wives. Outdo him if you will, but don't so much as glance at that Mayamohini whom Periya Pazhuvettaraiyan has married.'

'Thatha, I would never do such a terrible thing. I would never let down the Chozha and Malayaman clans like that!'

'Then why have you indulged her request, kuzhandaai?'

'I'll tell you the truth before I go, thatha. I have committed a grave crime against her. I'm going there to ask her forgiveness,' Karikalan said.

'What a thing to say! You want to ask a *woman* for forgiveness? Oh, I cannot bear to hear such a thing!'

Aditya Karikalan stared at the ground for a while. Then he found the strength to tell his grandfather the whole story. He told him of how he had searched out Veerapandiyan and found his hiding spot, how Nandini had put herself in his path and begged for mercy as he was about to attack Veerapandiyan, how he had ignored her and beheaded him in a rage, and how he had known no peace since.

'I cannot stop reliving this, thatha! I will not be able to put my heart at rest until I beg her forgiveness. It appears from her letter that she is ready to bury the past. And she seems keen to avoid a conflict over the administration of the empire. That is why she has urged me to come. I will finish my work there very soon and return right away to Kanchi. I will then set sail to find my brother and bring him back,' Aditya Karikalan said.

Malayaman sighed sorrowfully and said, 'A lot of things that didn't make sense thus far, do now. Things that were a mystery to me now have meaning. It is true that no one can defeat destiny.'

4

THE AYYANAAR TEMPLE

Even as grandfather and grandson were sitting on the bank of the Kedilam river and speaking to each other, our old friends Azhvarkadiyaan and Vandiyadevan were engaged in a strange undertaking in the town of Tirukaanaattumullur on the northern bank of the Kollidam.

Back in the day, the Kollidam was considered a holy river, like the Kaveri. It was said that during the Thulamaadam[1], Shiva would journey from the Kaanaattumullur temple in the form of Irapaadoorar[2] and bless the devotees who had gathered for a holy dip in the river.

During the afternoons of the Aippasi month, one would think a festival was on. People would come in hordes, even from the villages nearby.

The Vishnu temple of the town was small, but Vaishnavites believed their god too would descend to the river on his vaahan Garuda and bless them.

So it was not only Shaivites who came to the river.

Now, Azhvarkadiyaan elbowed his way to the middle of this throng, stuck a naaval branch into the ground and shouted, 'Naavalo Naaval! Naavalo Naaval! I'm here for a debate. I will defend the view that Vaishnavism is the greatest religion on Naaval Theevu[3]! Shaivites, Shaaktas[4], Advaitas, Kapalikas, Kalamukhas, Buddhists, Jains, whoever wishes may engage in debate with me. I will carry whoever defeats me on my shoulders in procession around the town. If they lose, they will have to give me everything on them but for their waistcloths! Naavalo Naaval!'

Rudraksha malas, makara pendants, kamandalus, kundalams[5], silk pitambaras, gold coins were all heaped before him. It was clear that he had defeated many opponents in debate. Vandiyadevan was toying with a dagger, leaning against a kadamba tree near Azhvarkadiyaan. He wore nothing but a waistcloth and had nothing in his hands save for the dagger. He gave the impression of being Azhvarkadiyaan's henchman, a knife-wielding bodyguard as it were.

A group of Shaivites approached them, shouting loudly.

Vandiyadevan roared in a stentorian voice, 'Be warned! The debate must be fair. If anyone so much as lays a finger on the Vaishnavite, you will be this dagger's next target!'

He flipped the dagger a couple of times, and the angry Shaivites decided it was prudent to calm down.

'O Vaishnavane!' one of them called. 'Don't think the world of yourself because you've won a few debates here! Go to Tirunaaraiyur! Our Nambiyaandaar Nambi will defeat you so soundly in argument that you will run in humiliation from the spot!'

'Ask your Tirunaaraiyur Nambi to come to Tirunarayanapuram and engage in debate with Anand Bhattar! There's a fair chance I'll be there too,' Azhvarkadiyaan said.

Although he cried, 'Naavalo Naaval!' multiple times after, he found no new takers.

So, he removed the naaval branch and replaced it with a white flag bearing the conch and discus emblems of Vaishnavism to indicate that he had won.

Immediately, a group of Vaishnavites gathered around him, hoisted him onto their shoulders and took him on a victory lap, crying:

Narayanane nam deivam
Naamellaarum thuthi seivam!

Narayana alone is our lord,
And we will all sing his praises!

Then, several of them said, 'Veera Vaishnavane! Please grace our homes with your presence and partake of a meal.'

'As you wish,' Azhvarkadiyaan said.

He and Vandiyadevan went from house to house, downing pots of puliyorai, payasam and dudyonam,

Azhvarkadiyaan gave a pitambaram to Vandiyadevan for use as an angavastram, and distributed the rest among the Vaishnavites, saying he had no use for goods, and only needed gold coins to journey to Haridwar. They plied him with more gold than all the goods were worth.

By afternoon, he and Vandiyadevan were on their way to Kadambur with the money.

Why had they staged this whole gig when they were in a hurry to carry a message?

Because, when they had arrived at the Kollidam, the volume of water and the speed of the current had been too much for them to traverse on horseback. So, they'd had to leave their horses behind and go by boat. Their boat had been rather too full, and capsized near the opposite shore. Vandiyadevan had been forced to swim to safety like everyone else. In the process, he had lost the waistcloth in which he had secured the various seals and signet rings he carried, the scroll Ilaiya Piraatti had given him and the gold coins he had been carrying, all of which he had safeguarded through so many hazards. They had all disappeared in the current.

Needing money to procure fresh horses, Azhvarkadiyaan and Vandiyadevan had come up with a plan. The plan worked, but there were no horses to be had in the rural areas they passed. There was a weekly market in Kadambur and Vandiyadevan thought they might find horses for sale there. If not, they would have to go all the way to Tirupaadirippuliyur.

The two friends weighed the pros and cons of going to Kadambur. They might hear news of Aditya Karikalan there, perhaps learn whether he was coming to the palace or not. Had he left Kanchi? Which route had he taken? They might find out all this. But there were other dangers in Kadambur. They had to avoid anyone who might recognise them. If they were to run into Kandamaaran, they would be in trouble. And if the Pazhuvoor entourage had arrived, that would pose a problem too.

'Vaishnavane! You're an expert at scaling walls in the dark, no? Why don't you steal a couple of horses from Sambuvarayar's stables?' Vandiyadevan suggested.

'I can scale walls all right. But how will the horses I steal do that?' Azhvarkadiyaan retorted.

'If the Pazhuvoor soldiers have arrived, we can take off with two of theirs. They tormented my horse in Kadambur, remember? I must avenge that!' the Vaanar scion said.

This prompted them to discuss the events of the evening they had first met, all those months ago, and the midnight conference they had espied from different vantage points.

They reached Kadambur by sundown. The entire town was in commotion. Flags and decorations ornamented every gate of the palace. The patrol had been boosted along the city walls and the palace fort. The crown prince was arriving after all.

His entourage, along with the Pazhuvoor entourage, would ensure that the town was busy all night. The people were also keen to see the Pazhuvoor Ilaiya Rani, who was due to arrive with her husband.

The two friends heard the townsfolk speaking about these developments as they passed through the main street. They also learnt that neither entourage had arrived yet and that Sambuvarayar's son Kandamaaran had gone to invite Aditya Karikalar personally and escort him to Kadambur. Some people whispered among themselves about Arulmozhi Varmar, who had 'drowned at sea'. Many of them seemed unhappy about a feast and celebration being organised when such a sorrowful event had occurred.

Azhvarkadiyaan and Vandiyadevan eavesdropped on all this while pretending they weren't listening. Neither wished to stay the night in Kadambur. Surely, they would find a place where they could sleep outside the town, an abandoned ruin if nothing else? If they couldn't, they would go to Veeranarayanapuram for the night and sleep at the temple. They could both do with a good night's sleep.

They crossed the town soon enough. A little further down the road, they saw a bamboo forest. There was an Ayyanaar temple there.

'Vaishnavare, I can't walk anymore. Let's stay the night here. This is a good place to stay hidden,' Vandiyadevan said. 'We won't meet a soul here.'

'Appane! You're wrong. What if someone else shows up, to stay the night like us?' Azhvarkadiyaan asked.

'It would suit us well if they turned up with horses.'

'No horse can walk through this bamboo forest. It's no easy task even for people.'

'There must be a footpath somewhere. The temple priest has to get there, no?'

The two men searched through the thick bamboo shoots and eventually found the footpath. They had a hard time avoiding the bamboo thorns as they passed through. They finally arrived at the clearing where the Ayyanaar temple was located. There was a slab meant for animal sacrifices. Next to the slab was a row of clay horses and elephants. It was customary for devotees to offer horses or elephants of clay to Ayyanaar.

'We were worried about horses,' Vandiyadevan said. 'Why don't we ask Ayyanaar's permission to take a couple of these?'

'Haven't you heard the proverb "Mann kuthirayai nambi aatril iranaga koodaadhu"—You must never get into a river placing your trust on a clay horse?' Azhvarkadiyaan said.

'Vaishnavane! Our Ayyanaar is a powerful god. He grants us our wishes immediately, not like your Vishnu who sleeps through the day while his devotees suffer,' Vandiyadevan said.

'In that case, your Ayyanaar might breathe life into these mud horses, no? Excellent, we'll save some money too.'

'A true devotee can certainly win that boon from him. For that matter, Brahma is supposed to have created us from clay, no?'

'True, thambi, we forget that we're all made of clay. That is why Vaishnavite acharyas ask us to smear "tirumann"[6] on our bodies.'

Vandiyadevan suddenly shushed Azhvarkadiyaan and held his arm. He pointed at something with his free hand.

It was dark. In the dim moonlight that filtered down through the bamboo shoots, it appeared the clay animals were moving. An elephant and a horse were drawing away from each other. Vandiyadevan looked on in disbelief. Not wanting to lose an opportunity to marvel at Ayyanaar's divine powers to Azhvarkadiyaan, he opened his mouth to goad him, when the Vaishnavite grasped his arm and gestured with a finger to his lips. Azhvarkadiyaan then pulled him into hiding, behind a bamboo shoot.

A human head was peeping out from the gap between the clay elephant and horse. It looked this way and that. It was a frightening sight, a disembodied head appearing right next to the sacrificial slab. Vandiyadevan, who had witnessed the most horrific sights on various battlefields, found his teeth chattering when he saw the revolving head. However, Azhvarkadiyaan's hand was steady. Perhaps there was a rational explanation, Vandiyadevan thought.

As they watched, the human head rose and revealed a torso. And then, a man stepped out. It appeared there was a tunnel hidden behind the clay animals.

They soon identified the man. He was none other than Idumbankaari, who was spying for Ravidasan while working as one of the Kadambur palace staff. Vandiyadevan and Azhvarkadiyaan looked at each other in surprise when they realised who he was.

Idumbankaari left the door of the tunnel open. After taking another look around, he made for the Ayyanaar temple. He opened the door. Soon, there was a glow from inside the temple. He must have lit a lamp.

'Thambi, what do you make of this?' Azhvarkadiyaan whispered.

'It strikes me that Ayyanaar is a powerful god. Didn't you see the clay horse come to life?'

'Yeah, sure. But what do you think of the man who has just arrived?'

'He must be the temple priest. Shall we go and pray?'

'Hold on, let's see if someone else comes to join us in prayer.'

'Do you think more people will show up?'

'Why else would he have lit the lamp?'

'Why wouldn't a temple priest light the lamp?'

'Thambi, do you really not see who he is'?'

'Of course I do. The man who brought me a horse on the south bank of the Kollidam, Idumbankaari. Perhaps I should ask him for a horse now.'

'What a brilliant idea ...'

'Why, you don't like it?'

'Idumbankaari is not just the man who brought you a horse. He's also one of Ravidasan's men.'

'In that case, I have another brilliant idea.'

'Do tell.'

'While he's busy with his priestly duties, maybe I should go see where Idumbankaari came from. Where does the tunnel go and so on?'

'How will you do that?'

'Why can't I enter the place from which he exited?'

'You can, but there might be danger lurking inside ...'

'Is there any place without danger lurking inside?'

'Well, up to you then!'

'Vaishnavare! You stay here and keep a watch on what happens.'

'Sure, no problem. Do you have any thoughts on where the tunnel is likely to lead?'

'I do, swami, I do. I just want to make sure I'm right.'

'Why?'

'Who knows when it might come in handy?'

They could hear more voices some distance away.

'Okay, I can't delay this any longer. You'll wait here until I return, won't you? You won't do to me as Sugreeva did to Vaali, will you?'

'I'll stay here as long as I live. But how can I be sure you'll return?'

'As long as I'm alive, I will.'

With this, Vandiyadevan dashed to the spot from which Idumbankaari had emerged. He disappeared into the hole. It was as if the mouth of the tunnel had swallowed him.

Idumbankaari now emerged from the temple and looked around. He noticed that the entrance to the tunnel had been left open. He went up to the sacrificial slab and moved the trishul. It acted as a lever and closed the entrance, bringing the horse and elephant back to their original positions.

Then, Idumbankaari stood waiting at the temple steps. Soon, Ravidasan, Soman Saambavan and the rest arrived from elsewhere.

Azhvarkadiyaan shrank further back into the shoots.

Ravidasan took his seat on the temple steps, and the others sat on the floor before him.

'My friends! The time is nearly upon us to fulfil the oath we swore,' Ravidasan said.

'We've been saying that for six months now,' one of the men said.

'Yes, and it's true enough. The day has been nearing us for six months. But now, we can count on our fingers the number of days left until we fulfil our oath. News has reached confirming that Aditya Karikalan has left Kanchi. The old man from Tirukkovalur tried to dissuade him, but his efforts came to nothing.'

'How do we know that nobody else will meet him on the way and succeed in dissuading him?'

'Aditya Karikalan will not step back once he has set out. He won't listen to anyone else.'

'What if the message his sister has sent reaches him?'

'How will it reach? We tied up the messenger in the forest, didn't we?'

'Tied him up, indeed! I saw him just today, on the northern bank of the Kollidam. Another of our enemies was there too.'

'Who?'

'That Vaishnavite fraud.'

'Then we must be careful. We must make sure they don't meet Aditya Karikalan.'

'How stupid that we must go to all this trouble, after having already caught him! Why did the Rani ask us to let him go?'

'I didn't understand at first. Then, I realised. I admit the Rani is even cleverer than I am. There is a very important reason for her wanting Vandiyadevan alive. There is no need for you to know that right now. Don't worry yourselves about Vandiyadevan. But if any of you sees that Vaishnavite, don't hesitate to kill him,' Ravidasan said.

5

A FRIGHTENING CELLAR

Vandiyadevan entered the secret passage and found he had to take some steps that led further down. He finally arrived at a level floor. There was hardly any light. He walked a few feet, and then he heard a grinding noise, as if wheels were turning. All of a sudden, it became pitch dark. How many times had he sworn not to intervene in things that did not concern him, he wondered.

What an important mission he had set out on! He had postponed that to enter this subterranean passage. Where was it going to lead him? Into what new peril? What a stupid undertaking this was! When would his impulsiveness and haste stop impeding him?

These thoughts slowed his feet. Perhaps he was better off returning to Azhvarkadiyaan. He found the steps and climbed back up, but no light shone from above. The door was closed. He groped what was now the ceiling, but to no avail. Someone must have closed the entrance.

Sweat was pouring down his face and back. He made another, urgent attempt to open the door. Then, he heard voices that sounded as if they were coming from far away. Someone must have arrived at the Ayyanaar temple, he thought. Multiple voices. More than one person then. Idumbankaari had lit the lamp expecting company.

If the conspirators had gathered there, it would be a huge mistake to emerge from the hidden door. Who knew how long they would stay there? If it was indeed Ravidasan with the rest of them, they might talk for a good while. Why had they come here? And what were they speaking about? Were they plotting some new evil? The Veeravaishnavan would listen in, he was sure. It made more sense for Vandiyadevan to explore the cellar than to stand there sweating and panting. Now that he had entered it, he might as well find out where it ended.

He went back the way he had come. The floor was level, but not even. The cellar must have been hewn from rock. Surely, this must be a secret passage that originated in the Kadambur Sambuvarayar Palace? Where in the palace? It could be the treasury. Or the antapuram where the royal women lived. He knew that all palaces had such secret tunnels through which the royals could escape in case of danger. Since it was most important to secure the women and the treasure, the secret passages typically led out from those points.

Since Idumbankaari had emerged from there, it was more likely that the passage would lead to the treasury. Perhaps the conspirators were helping themselves to Sambuvarayar's valuables, as they were to Pazhuvettaraiyar's. But why had they chosen this time, when Aditya Karikalar and several suzerain kings were going to stay at the palace, for such a discreet undertaking? Perhaps it was not to steal valuables, but for something else entirely?

Vandiyadevan thought back to the conversation he had overheard at the Tiruppurambiyam pallipadai. Then he thought of the lethal sword the Pazhuvoor Ilaiya Rani held so dear. His hair stood on end. What if they were on a far more terrible mission than theft? If he could ascertain where the passage ended, it might help him avert whatever disaster lay in wait.

It had only been a few minutes since he had entered the passage. But the dark and the stuffiness made him feel he had been in there for much longer. He was sweating from the lack of ventilation. He felt rather lightheaded too. He tried to calculate the distance between the palace and the Ayyanaar temple. His heart sank when he realised how far it was. Then, he thought again. It was quite a distance if one went by the grand entrance of the palace and made one's way through the street. However, it was not far from the back of the palace. Perhaps within shooting distance of an arrow. If that were the case, he must have reached the walls of the fort by now …

Yes, it must be right, for a jet of air hit him from above. Vandiyadevan, who had been feeling faint from the heat and lack of air, felt rejuvenated by it. He looked up. Far above his head, he could make out a small hole that let in a shaft of light. He could hear distant voices too. There were several bastions around the fort walls, for the soldiers who patrolled them. The passage must have been cut so that air entered it from holes hewed into some of these bastions. However, there was no provision for anyone to climb into or out of the passage at these points.

The idea that he had found a way into the palace, along with the relief from the air, energised Vandiyadevan. It wouldn't be long before he was in the room where the passage ended. The treasury, perhaps? Could Sambuvarayar have heaped pearls and corals and diamonds and gold and precious gems as Pazhuvettaraiyar had? Was he likely to find a human skeleton here too? Would spiderwebs have wound themselves around heaps of gold coins here too?

Distracted by his thoughts, Vandiyadevan tripped. It was with some relief that he realised that he had tripped on a step. A stairway now led upwards. At the top, he was sure to find the treasury. If not, it would lead into the antapuram. Well, that could be embarrassing. Kandamaaran's sister Manimeghalai would be there! He thought about how he had once aspired to marry that dusky beauty. It amused him now. There was no one to appreciate his grin. What if he were to enter the antapuram when the women were lolling about, secure in their privacy… what a shock they would get! The idea was so hilarious he laughed out loud, just as he arrived on the top step.

The very next moment, his blood froze. His eyes nearly popped out. Before him was a truly terrible sight.

As he had arrived at the top step, he had looked about himself, still laughing. A hundred eyes stared back at him. They were all the eyes of wild animals.

His first instinct was to turn and run back down the stairs. But he could not find them! The floor was level about him. He now recalled that he had heard a sliding sound as he had reached the top step. There must be some provision that sealed off the tunnel once one had arrived at the palace.

But what was this assembly of animals? It was as if the entire fauna population of the forest had gathered to attack him. There were tigers, leopards, lions, bears, wild buffaloes, wolves, jackals, rhinoceros, and … two elephants! And what an enormous kite! Aiyo! A giant owl! And was that a bat? Was he having a nightmare? Surely this could not be real, for in the middle of all this was a crocodile, jaws open as if ready for prey! But then … none of them had attacked him, and this crocodile should be in the water, not land! How had it …

Phew! He was saved! He realised all these animals were no longer alive. They were hunting trophies. He now recalled Kandamaaran having once told him how his clan was fond of hunting and how they had dedicated a hall to display stuffed animals they had killed. He must have reached that hall then.

Although he knew he was safe now, his body was still trembling from the initial shock.

It took some time for him to recover, and then his habitual curiosity took over. He went close to the animals. He touched some of them, shook others. Well, it was clear that none was alive. He then wondered what his next course of action should be. His entry point could not serve as the exit because it had shut on its own. Should he search for a way to open it? Or should he see where this hall led? Or should he check if there was another room that opened off this one, aside from the main door that must lead to one of the palace corridors?

He went around the hall, checking if there was a door anywhere in the walls. When he didn't find a regular door, he knocked his fists against the walls to check if there was any hollow portion and felt about with his hands. Nothing. As time went by, he found himself getting angry. Why had he got himself into this mess? He then noticed the head of an elephant with its trunk and tusks, embedded into the wall.

'Cursed elephant! It was one of your ilk that moved and tempted me to go down this passage!' he scolded the head.

The elephant did not respond. Elephants did not usually speak, even when alive. Dead elephants could not be expected to respond. This one did not so much as move its trunk.

'Can't you hear me ask you questions? Why do you stay silent?' demanded Vandiyadevan. He reached out and twisted one of the elephant's tusks.

The next moment, something magical happened.

The ears of the elephant waved and then moved, carrying the head sideways. There in the wall was a door! Vandiyadevan pushed the door lightly and peeked inside.

He saw a woman's face. A young woman, with a dark complexion and beautiful features. Her large eyes widened in surprise as she saw him. And then! What was this? He saw his own face appear next to hers. Why, he was positioned as a lover about to kiss her cheek! Her eyes grew even wider, as if she was not just surprised but also scared now. She was still for a moment, and then her red lips let out a high-pitched, 'Kooooooo!'

Vandiyadevan was so shocked he let go of the elephant's tusk. The next moment, the door had disappeared and the elephant's head was back in place. There was no young woman and the echo of her scream stopped ringing in his ears.

His heart was hammering.

The woman's face … what did it mean?

6

MANIMEGHALAI

Sambuvarayar's beloved daughter Manimeghalai was a cheerful presence, filled with the confidence of a girl who'd had an idyllic childhood, and had known the warmth and affection of both her parents as well as her brother Kandamaaran throughout her growing years. In the palace, her word was law. She might as well have held the royal sceptre. Until recently, her life had been filled with song and dance and celebration. It was only a few months ago that she had encountered the first obstacle to continued joy. The elders of the house had insisted she do something that went against her wishes. She did her best to show them that they could not succeed in forcing her hand, but her efforts had little effect.

Over the last couple of years, every time Kandamaaran returned from the battlefield, he had spoken of his friend Vallavarayan Vandiyadevan. He had praised his courage and acuity to the skies.

Kandamaaran had said his friend's looks could give Manmadha a run for his money, his skills matched Arjuna's, while his foresight and strategic planning could rival Krishna's.

'He would make the perfect husband for you. He'll know how to deal with your audacity and keep you in check,' Kandamaaran would say.

Manimeghalai would long to hear of Vandiyadevan, although she pretended to be annoyed with Kandamaaran for going on and on about him.

'This is all just talk. Why don't you bring him here one day so I can see for myself?' she would demand.

'As you wish, as you wish,' Kandamaaran would promise.

Manimeghalai had brought Vandiyadevan to life in her dreamworld. She saw him in her mind's eye and fantasised about conversations with him, their jokes and antics, and of the fights they would have and the way they would make up after. Daydreams began to intrude into her life. She would laugh with her close friends about her brother's beloved friend, and they would tease her about him. But about four months ago, something entirely unexpected happened, threatening to shatter these dreams.

Kandamaaran began to sing a different tune all of a sudden. 'Forget that orphan who has no home or title or wealth!' he began to say. She could one day sit on the throne of Thanjavur, he said. One fine day, he made the grand reveal. He said he wanted to marry her off to Madurantakan, who had already taken Chinna Pazhuvettaraiyar's daughter for his first wife. Madurantakan would be the next emperor, he hinted. If Manimeghalai were to marry him, she would be the empress who ruled the three worlds, and one of the sons she bore him could one day become the chakravarti of the Chozha empire. Her parents too sang harmonies to his song.

But Manimeghalai was disturbed by this talk. She had lost her heart to Vandiyadevan, after hearing about him all these years. Besides, she knew that Madurantakan had never been to the battlefield. He had the reputation of being a coward. And all this while, he had covered his body in vibhuti and his chest with rudraksha beads and had gone on about wanting to take to ascetism and devote himself to the worship of Shiva. As if all this were not deterrent enough, he was already married. The women of the Thanjavur Palace were known to be arrogant. They believed they were the only cultured women in the empire, and that everyone from other towns was inferior to them. Taking all this into consideration, Manimeghalai grew increasingly resentful of her family. She refused to acquiesce. Forget the throne of Thanjavur, she wouldn't marry Madurantakan even if she were going to sit as his consort on the throne of Devaloka.

And when another piece of news filtered down, her resolution only grew stronger. When Periya Pazhuvettaraiyar visited the Kadambur Palace during the month of Adi, they heard that he was accompanied by the Ilaiya Rani Nandini Devi. But she did not come to the antapuram. She did not so much as meet the women of the Kadambur Palace. At first, the women were surprised. Then, they began to speak of the Pazhuvoor Rani with contempt and scorn, mocking her choice of husband and the considerations that had led to that choice. Eventually, they learnt the truth. It was not the Pazhuvoor Rani who had arrived in the palanquin, but Madurantaka Devar.

The thought of a man travelling in the palanquin disgusted Manimeghalai. *Chhi chhi! How can I marry a man who would disguise himself as a woman?*

And it was when this thought was running through her head that Vandiyadevan visited the palace for the first time, arriving at the same time as Madurantakan. Her brother's friend didn't stay long at the antapuram, but Manimeghalai found herself overcome with shyness throughout the duration of his interaction with the women. She hid behind the others. She wasn't able to meet Vandiyadevan's eyes. Why, she couldn't even bring herself to look at his face. But she did steal the odd glance while she was concealed behind her companions. His twinkling eyes and handsome countenance etched themselves into her heart. His deep voice and his cheerful repartee played over and over again in her ears.

And so began an endless argument between Manimeghalai and her brother. Forget her family, not even Lord Shiva with his three eyes would succeed in commanding her to marry Madurantakan, she said. She also made it clear that even in the short time she had seen Vandiyadevan, she had accepted him as her one true love.

This infuriated Kandamaaran.

He tried sweet-talking her out of this decision at first. When that did not work, he said, 'Vandiyadevan is not my friend. He is my greatest enemy. He tried to stab me to death when my back was turned. If you insist on marrying him, I will kill both of you with my own hands!'

He showed her the wound on his back. He said the only reason he had survived the attack was the love and care the Pazhuvoor Ilaiya Rani had showered on him as he was recovering.

'If you have the slightest trust in me, forget a man called Vandiyadevan ever existed!'

Once she learnt of the stabbing, Manimeghalai did have a change of heart. She adored her brother. It was true that she could not marry a man who had attempted to murder him. And so, she did her best to overcome her feelings for Vandiyadevan. But this was no easy undertaking. All too often, when she least expected it, the smile that danced across his lips would appear before her eyes. His face appeared both in her dreams and her daydreams.

These were the reasons for Manimeghalai losing her natural cheeriness over the last few months. She was plagued by sorrow and exhaustion. The elders believed the change in her demeanour was due to her being of marriageable age. Her companions teased her about her impending marriage. Those who sensed something was wrong tried to cheer her up with fun and games. Nothing had the intended effect.

However, she regained some of her spirit after learning that her brother and parents had abandoned their plan of marrying her off to Madurantakan. She heard them whispering about the emperor's eldest son and heir Aditya Karikalar being a prospective groom instead.

There was no man or woman in all of Tamizhagam who had not heard of Aditya Karikalar's battlefield heroics. Everyone was also aware that he had been refusing marriage for some reason. What a stroke of luck it would be to marry such a prince! Every princess from every royal family across the kingdoms of the peninsula was dreaming of such an alliance. Was she, Manimeghalai, really to be the lucky one? The thought rejuvenated her.

She then learnt that Aditya Karikalar was making his way to the Kadambur Palace from Kanchi, while Periya Pazhuvettaraiyar was heading there from Thanjavur. This time round, he was indeed bringing his wife along. Nandini Devi had saved Manimeghalai's brother's life. He couldn't stop speaking about her beauty and kindness and intelligence. He had also told Manimeghalai that it was the Pazhuvoor Ilaiya Rani who had initiated the alliance with Aditya Karikalar. Kandamaaran was keen for his sister to be Nandini Devi's constant companion during her stay and impress her as an impeccable hostess. Manimeghalai was all set. She would become close friends with the Pazhuvoor Ilaiya Rani, and then learn everything she needed to so as to ensure she outdid the women of the Thanjavur Palace where grace and manners and culture and sophistication were concerned.

In the week leading up to the arrival of the guests, Manimeghalai was in a tizzy, supervising the arrangements in the palace and ensuring that everything was perfect. She was particularly anxious that the Pazhuvoor Ilaiya Rani's quarters should have every luxury that befitted Nandini Devi. Her brother had told her how important it was that she made a good impression on Nandini Devi. And so, she put the servants' noses to the grindstone. She tested the patience of her friends and companions, making them arrange and rearrange every bit of furniture and ornamentation in the Pazhuvoor Ilaiya Rani's quarters.

She also kept her eye on the rooms reserved for Prince Aditya Karikalar and his friends. Someone called Parthibendran was said to be coming along. Who knew what he would be like? And who knew which way anyone's loyalties would turn? Her brother's former friend Vandiyadevan was among Aditya Karikalar's dearest friends and would certainly have been part of his entourage if he had not betrayed Kandamaaran as he had. Yes, this is how it went … whatever else she busied herself with, Manimeghalai couldn't keep her thoughts from turning to the man who had been such a treacherous friend to her brother.

The Pazhuvoor Rani was expected to reach that very night. And so, Manimeghalai was supervising the last-minute arrangements in her rooms. She happened to stand before the mirror that had been placed in a corner of the wall for the benefit of Nandini Devi. Manimeghalai studied her own reflection. She told herself that her face lacked nothing for beauty. As she was about to move away from the mirror, another face appeared in the reflection. This face was so close to her own, they were a hair's breadth away from touching cheeks. It was the face that haunted her dreams and daydreams, the face of the Vaanar scion.

Her mouth involuntarily opened and let out a gasp of surprise.

The next moment, her face was the only one in the mirror. The other face had disappeared.

7

THE TAILLESS MONKEY

Manimeghalai was lost in thought for some time. Had she imagined the form she had just seen? Or had it been a dream? If it had been a dream, she should have been asleep ... she must still be asleep. She pinched herself. No, she was not asleep. This was the room that was being readied for Pazhuvoor Ilaiya Rani Nandini Devi's stay. There, she could see her reflection clearly in the mirror. There, the kuththuvilakku was burning bright.

She squinted at the wall facing the mirror. She knew there was a secret passage that lay behind it. The door could be opened both from inside and outside. She went to the point from where the door slid out, pressed her ear to the wall and listened closely. The hidden door was made of wood. She thought she heard some noise in the adjoining room, the one with the hunting trophies.

Manimeghalai gently opened the hidden door. She peeped into the trophy room. Most of it was plunged in darkness. In one corner was a little oil lamp. For a moment, the flame dimmed and then shone again brightly. She thought she saw a figure slide past the lamp. The movement must have made the flame flicker. Was this the same person she had seen in the mirror? Or was she imagining this figure too?

The princess now clapped her hands and called softly, 'Who goes there?'

She heard the sound of a throat being cleared.

The only figure that moved was a bat, which switched its perch on the roof of the room for another spot.

And then, a soft cough.

Manimeghalai, standing at the door, called loudly, 'Adiye, Chandramati!'

'Yes, amma?'

'Bring a lamp and come here right away!'

Her maid arrived with a lamp.

'Why, this place is well-lit! Why did you ask for a lamp, amma?' the maid asked.

'We must go check the trophy room. I heard a noise there.'

'It must have been a bat flapping its wings, amma! What else could it have been?'

'No, di! I was looking into the mirror just now. Another face appeared right next to mine!'

'How did that face look? Like Manmadha? Or like Arjuna?' the maid asked, and began to laugh.

'What is this, Chandramati? Are you mocking me?'

'No, amma, no! You said you dream about him often, don't you? Was it perhaps he who appeared in the mirror now?'

'Yes, Chandramati! But this time, it seemed too real to be a dream.'

'Every woman is prone to such a hallucination, amma. This will last only a couple of days in your case. Once the prince arrives from Kanchi, you'll forget that old face.'

'Be that as it may, let's go into the trophy room and see what the matter is. Come on!'

'It would be a waste of time, amma. The trophy room is all dusty and dirty. Your clothes will be ruined.'

'So what?'

'You might start coughing and sneezing, right before the guests arrive tomorrow …'

'So what? We must search the trophy room right away! Carry the lamp carefully. Make sure the flame doesn't go out.'

With those words, Manimeghalai stepped into the trophy room, followed by her maid. They walked about the room. Chandramati stared at the lifeless animals mounted on the wall. Manimeghalai's attention was on the floor. She could see footprints in the dust.

'Amma, there!' Chandramati gasped.

'What happened? Why did you panic?'

'There! That tailless monkey seemed to move just now!'

'Perhaps it was so overjoyed to see you, it had to jump up and down?'

'Why are you making fun of me, amma?'

'Didn't you make fun of me, saying I was hallucinating?'

'Perhaps the face you saw in the mirror was that of the monkey! It is right across from the door, don't you see? There, the monkey is moving again.'

'Chhi, chhi! That's the shadow the lamp is casting! That gives us the illusion of the monkey moving. There is nobody here!'

'Then, it must have been the monkey's face that you saw in the mirror. Or perhaps that of the owl sitting up there. Look how it stares at us!'

'Why share the credit with me? It must be your beauty that's captivated the owl. It is so besotted with you that it cannot even blink!'

'In that case, who was staring at you in the mirror?'

'Adiye! You seem to have decided I was hallucinating. The face I so often see in my dreams was the one that appeared in the mirror. Just my luck that the eyes that fell on that handsome face must also take in this monkey and owl! Come, let's go back. Let me see if I can find that face in the mirror again!'

The two women retraced their steps into the antapuram.

Vandiyadevan stepped out from behind the tailless monkey.

He sneezed a few times to rid himself of the dust that had gone up his nose. He then thanked the monkey that had done such an excellent job of concealing him.

'O monkey! Long may you live! That maid compared my face to yours. That annoyed me so much I considered stepping out. Thankfully, I was able to check myself in time. If it hadn't been for you, standing there, the height of a man, what would have become of me? I would have been caught by those two! O monkey, may you stay blessed!'

As he came to the end of his oration, it struck him that it might not have been such a terrible fate if he had been caught by those two women. He had figured out who they were already. He had heard their conversation too. And it seemed to him that Manimeghalai was making a point of speaking as loudly as she could. What did she say about a face that appeared in her dreams? And how it was the same face she had seen in the mirror?

He was suddenly assailed by old memories. Kandamaaran had told Vandiyadevan how he had talked up his friend to his sister. The last time Vandiyadevan had visited this palace, he had seen her blushing behind the other women of the antapuram. But then, Kandamaaran had said she was going to be married off to someone else. Was this silly girl still thinking of him, though?

Well, there was no time to contemplate all that. He needed to find a way out of here now. The elephant tusk opened the door to the antapuram, and so it would be of no use now. He would have to find an exit point that would lead him back the way he had come. He knew the mechanisms that opened the doors would vary, depending on whether one was opening them from inside or outside. He could figure that out eventually, but he would have to find the door first. However much he stared at the walls, he couldn't make out where the door was. And the dimness of the room made it all the more difficult.

Then, he remembered that there had been a crocodile near the point from which he had entered. Perhaps if he went to that spot and tapped the wall, he would find the door that led out?

With this in mind, he marched up to the crocodile in question and felt the wall. He felt every inch of it, to no avail. As time passed, he grew more flustered. What a pain this was! He had got himself thoroughly trapped. Kadavule! It appeared his only option was to get out through the antapuram. But who knew what dangers awaited him if he went to the antapuram?

There was a chance Manimeghalai would be sympathetic to his cause. But what cause was that? What excuse would he offer for having entered the antapuram through a secret passage?

'I'm here because I'm so in love with you I just had to see you!' he could say … but what a cruel lie that would be! And even if he did tell her such a lie, would she believe him?

Then again, how could he be sure Manimeghalai would be alone? What if he walked into a gathering of women?

If Sambuvarayar came to know that he had sneaked into the women's quarters, he might well kill Vandiyadevan with his bare hands!

Vandiyadevan's attention was now drawn to the crocodile lying at his feet. And he found that he was angry with the dead animal.

'O crocodile, why are you holding your mouth open?' he demanded, and then aimed a kick at the dead animal.

The crocodile moved slightly when he kicked it. At the same time, a small gap appeared in the floor by the wall.

'Aha! So it was you who was hiding the way, eh? Stupid crocodile! Why didn't you tell me earlier?' Vandiyadevan asked, even as he bent down and pushed the crocodile to one side. As the crocodile moved, the opening grew wider and he saw a set of steps leading downwards.

8

TWO HANDS IN THE DARK

Vandiyadevan marvelled at how cleverly the entryways into the secret passages of the Kadambur Palace had been hidden. If someone who didn't know them like the back of his hand tried to hurriedly climb in or out, he could encounter grave danger. If the crocodile were to move when he was halfway down the stairs, he would be pinned to the wall. Vandiyadevan ensured that the crocodile was still before he put one foot through the door.

Ah! What was this now? He heard footsteps! Who could it be? Azhvarkadiyaan perhaps? Had he come in search of his friend? It was best to prevent his coming here ... no, no, wait, this wasn't a lone man. The footsteps indicated it was a group of at least five or six people. In that case, it could be Idumbankaari and his fellow conspirators. Vandiyadevan leapt into the air and landed right behind the tailless monkey again.

Oh, no! He had left the entryway into the secret passage open! Would they suspect something? No, no, this space had been open when he had arrived. It was only after he had stepped through the gap that it closed. So, it was a good thing it had remained open. There, a head was appearing through the entryway. It was indeed Idumbankaari. There, he had put one foot outside and was surveying the surroundings. He must be keeping one foot inside the gap so that the door would not close on him.

Adada! How bright it was here! Light was coming from the spot where the elephant's head was mounted on the wall. He could see it was opening into the antapuram. Who was coming out from there? Ah, it was Manimeghalai, carrying a lamp herself.

Idumbankaari jumped out of the gap, and the door to the passage way closed behind him. He pulled off the cloth he had wound around his head and hurriedly made a show of cleaning the dust off a tiger near him. How would this little drama end?

Manimeghalai held up the lamp and looked about herself. Once she spotted Idumbankaari, she began to walk towards him in surprise.

Idumbankaari stopped his dusting and looked at her with an equal measure of surprise.

'Thaaye! You, here? At this time? Whatever for?' he asked.

'Idumba! It's you, is it? What are you doing here?' Manimeghalai asked.

'Amma, the guests who are arriving tomorrow will have to be shown around the trophy room, won't they? So, I'm cleaning it properly. Chinna Ejamaan had instructed me to do this as he left for Kanchi.'

'Yes, Idumba, Chinna Ejamaan trusts only you and me in this entire palace. I was just making sure that all arrangements were in place in the quarters where the Pazhuvoor Rani will be housed. Then, I thought I heard a noise here and came to see what it was. I figured it must be you. No one else knows about this secret passage. How long have you been working here?'

'It must be more than one naazhigai, thaaye! I have another naazhigai's worth of work to finish. Did you come here all by yourself? Where is that chatterbox Chandramati?'

'I sent her to fetch my father because I heard a noise here. Now that I know it's only you, I'll go stop her.'

As she said this, Manimeghalai hoisted the lamp above her head and saw clearly the changes Idumbankaari's face underwent. Next, she turned her attention to the tailless monkey. She noticed that it was moving, as it had been before.

'Yes, thaaye. Ejamaan must have so much on his plate right now. Do stop her from worrying him and go rest up yourself. I'll take care of all the arrangements, please don't worry,' Idumbankaari said.

Manimeghalai returned the way she had come, and the portal into the antapuram vanished after her.

Idumbankaari went up to the elephant's head and pressed his ear to the wall. Once he had ascertained that there was no one in the adjoining room, he returned to the other secret door. He opened it and climbed down a couple of steps. An owl's hoot came from inside. Idumbankaari responded with a reciprocal hoot. Vandiyadevan could hear footsteps again.

And then, everything was happening all at once.

A bat rose into the air, flapping its wings. Idumbankaari turned to look at it. The tailless monkey collapsed on him from behind. Caught by surprise, his knees collapsed under the speed and weight of the falling monkey, and he staggered. The momentum forced him down a couple of more steps. Having no clue what had hit him, Idumbankaari screamed and started flailing his arms. Then, he realised it was the lifeless, tailless monkey. He fortified himself and tried to put the monkey back in its place.

By this time, two eyes appeared above him and it was as if a living man's arms were pushing him further down the stairwell. Idumbankaari couldn't believe it. For a moment, he was paralysed by fear. He looked up and down again. He noticed that the tailless monkey had fallen on him upside down, and that once half its body was down, the door had come closer. As for the human arms, those must have been a figment of his imagination.

His friends had joined him by now.

'Appane, what is this?' asked Ravidasan, who was leading the group. 'Why are you so flustered? Is there some danger about? Should we go back the way we came?'

'No, no, there's no danger. When I opened the door, that demon of a monkey somehow contrived to change its place and fall on me. I got scared for a moment. Now, the monkey is blocking the way, stuck without going up or down. Give me a minute, I'll clear the path for you.'

The readers must have figured out whose hands had reached down and pushed the stumbling Idumbankaari further down the stairwell. Vandiyadevan's luck did not desert him on this occasion either. The right strategy had occurred to him at the right time. With Idumbankaari staring after the flying bat, Vandiyadevan had found an opportune moment to push the tailless monkey onto him. Then, making sure his face couldn't be discerned, he had pushed Idumbankaari further down the stairs, and then sent the tailless monkey tumbling upside down after him. Last of all, he had moved the crocodile into place.

Having done all this in a flash, Vandiyadevan ran upto the elephant's head and twisted a tusk with all his might. An opening appeared in the wall. But this was not the spacious passage through which Manimeghalai had come. It was a round, narrow path. Perhaps it was a door within a door? How did one open the entire door? Well, there was no time to figure that out. The conspirators would enter the trophy room by then, and escaping from them would be near impossible.

So, it was best to go through the path that had opened, narrow as it was. Vandiyadevan put thought into action right away, and entered the orifice. His head, arms and half his body squeezed through the gap. But it was hard to get the rest past. There was no hold at the other end for him to lever himself down into the room either. At this point, the lamp in the room was extinguished and it became pitch dark.

Vandiyadevan called in a panicked voice, 'Chandramati! Chandramati! Save me!'

A peal of laughter sounded from within.

'Chandramati! You're right here, and you're laughing at me? You find this funny? Is that seemly?'

Another peal of laughter came in response, followed by a woman calling, 'What about your sneaking into the antapuram? Is *that* seemly?'

Vandiyadevan recognised Manimeghalai's voice. Yet, he said, 'Chandramati! I came only because you asked me to! I'm being pursued. Let me in, or there will be a mess!'

'Ah, Chandramati is that clever, is she? It's fine, I'll teach both of you a lesson!'

'Oho! You're Princess Manimeghalai, aren't you? Ammani! Please forgive me and save me just this once! I'll never make such a mistake again! You will earn great punyam[1] for this.'

Two slim hands reached out from the darkness, caught hold of Vandiyadevan's shoulders and gently lowered him down onto the floor. The hole in the wall disappeared.

'Ilavarasi! A million thanks to you!' he said.

'Hold on. Decide whether you want to thank me once you learn what I have in store for you!'

'You can do whatever you want to me! But you helped me escape from murderers, that's enough. If it were to happen that I am destined to die at your beautiful hands instead of those rakshasas', I would consider it my great good fortune!'

'Ade appa! You seem to be a great hero! Who are those murderers who are pursuing you? Hold on, let me light the lamp and get a look at your face!'

'Ammani! Must you see my face again? Why, the monkey face that appeared behind you as you were looking into the mirror is my very own! Chandramati gave you a description, no?' Vandiyadevan said.

The sound of laughter and the tinkling of bangles filled the dark of the room. When Vandiyadevan had pushed his head into the room, Manimeghalai had covered the lamp that was lighting the room. Now that she had lifted the lid from it, the lamp glowed in the dark. Upon seeing Vandiyadevan's face, Manimeghalai stood mesmerised. It was then that they heard the sound of several people running into the adjoining trophy room.

9

THE BARKING DOG

Manimeghalai stood looking at Vandiyadevan's face. Even as Vandiyadevan smiled, his mind was racing—what should he tell this girl and how could he escape?

At that moment, a voice called from some distance away, 'Amma! Did you call me?'

'No, di, go about your work!' Manimeghalai said.

She was no longer flustered. She walked over to the door from which Vandiyadevan had entered, and bolted it from inside. Then, she signalled to Vandiyadevan to come along, and took him to the other end of the room.

Then, she turned suddenly to him and asked, 'Aiya, please tell me the truth. You said Chandramati called you here. Is that really the case?'

'Yes, ammani!'

'In that case, when and where did she meet you and ask you to come here?'

'Oh, just a while ago. When I was hiding behind the monkey in the next room, the two of you came and took a look around. Once you had left, she looked at me and said, "O monkey, will you come and stay in my room? It would be a good way to scare off unwanted guests!" I guess you didn't hear her say that?'

Manimeghalai said with a little smile, 'If I had heard her say that, would I have let her get away with it?'

'Ilavarasi! What's the point of getting angry with your friend? What can Chandramati do about my face looking exactly like that of the tailless monkey?'

'Oh, your face looks nothing like that of the tailless monkey.'

'Then, perhaps it looks like that of the owl hanging above the monkey?'

'Your face is neither that of a monkey nor of an owl. But you've got all the tricks of the monkey in you. At times, you stare like an owl too. It *was* you who peeked into this mirror some time ago and stared, wasn't it?'

'Indeed, ilavarasi, it was.'

'Then, why did you look away and shut the door right after?'

'When I looked into the mirror, I saw a face that looked like that of a celestial apsara next to mine. I didn't want my face to frighten that apsara, and the thought distracted me into letting go of the elephant tusk I'd been holding. The door shut the moment I did that.'

'Do you know who that celestial apsara is?'

'I didn't know back then. But I gave it some thought and figured it out.'

'What did you figure out?'

'That the woman I saw was no celestial apsara, but whose feet all the celestial apsaras run to touch ... Manimeghalai Devi, the beloved daughter of Kadambur Sambuvarayar. It also struck me that she was the cherished sister of my dearest friend Kandamaaran.'

Manimeghalai's eyebrows came together in a frown. She asked, in a voice dripping with anger and sarcasm, 'Really? My brother is your dearest friend, is he?'

'Why would you doubt that, ilavarasi? I came here four months ago, don't you remember? I stayed the night. I even visited the antapuram to pay my respects to the elder women of the royal family. Don't you remember?'

'I remember all too well. How could one forget it in such a short time? The prince of the Vaanar clan, Vallavarayar Vandiyadevar, that's who you are. Yes?'

'Yes, ilavarase! I have no palace to live in and no kingdom to rule, and bear the clan's title of 'arayan', and I am indeed the pauper-prince you met. There was a time when your brother sang your praises to me. When Kandamaaran and I were serving on the guard at the banks of the Vadapennai river, he would often speak of you. I nurtured all sorts of dreams too. And then I let go of all those fantasies.'

A sudden thought occurred to Manimeghalai. Kandamaaran claimed this man had tried to stab him to death. Why would he have done such a thing to her brother? Could it have something to do with her? Perhaps he had got into a fight with Kandamaaran for refusing to give her to him in marriage? The thought stirred a storm of ecstasy in her heart. She turned that into a storm of fury and said, 'Aiya! There's no point in talking about the past. Tell me why you have sneaked into the palace today. Otherwise, I'll have to send for my friend and ask her to tell my father about this!'

'Ilavarasi! I have already told you the reason for my coming in here. I was being chased by a band of murderers. When I was running away from them, I saw a door in the ground. I realised it was some kind of secret passage. I decided to escape that way, and it led me here.'

'Aiya! You're the very embodiment of heroism. I have heard of any number of asayaha soorars—men who can overpower an army without help. But this is the first time I've met an ottathil soorar—a man who can outrun anyone. Why, Uttarakumaran[1] must bow down to you!'

This hit Vandiyadevan hard. Here was Manimeghalai, whom he'd taken for a silly girl, using sarcasm against him!

'Devi, they're a group of seven or eight. And I'm alone. They're armed, and I have no weapons on me.

My cherished spear was carried away by the waters of the Kollidam river.'

'Oh, that's good, very good! That cruel sinful spear that stabbed a friend in the back has been carried away by the river … that's very good!'

Vandiyadevan was startled out of his skin. Before he could open his mouth to respond, Manimeghalai said, 'Do tell me the truth. Have you come here to escape from murderers, or to commit a murder?'

Vandiyadevan jumped as if he had just stepped on fire. 'Shivashiva! Narayana! To kill whom would I come here? Would I kill my dear friend's beloved sister? Why?'

'How would I know? You say "dear friend" so easily. What a lie! Didn't you try to kill that dear friend by stabbing him in the back? You're perhaps here to kill someone else for the very same reason.'

'Kadavule! What an accusation! You say it was *I* who stabbed Kandamaaran in the back? I would have chopped off my hand rather than do such a thing! Ilavarasi! Who told you such an evil lie?'

'My brother himself told me. I would never have believed it if I'd heard it from anyone else.'

'Did Kandamaaran really say such a thing? Then, I'm truly cursed. Someone had stabbed him in the back and thrown him by the wall of the Thanjavur fortress. He was unconscious. I carried him to the hut of Senthan Amudan and saved his life. Is this my reward? Ilavarasi! Why would I try to kill him? Did he come up with any reason?'

'Indeed he did! I believe you said I'm most ugly, that the women of Thanjavur are far prettier than I. Kandamaaran got angry with you, and the two of you got into a fight. But instead of facing him in combat, you stabbed him in the back. Is all this true or not?'

'Lies! Lies! Terrible lies! I would have cut my tongue off rather than call you ugly! It was Kandamaaran who insisted that I should forget his sister ever existed, don't you know?'

'Why?'

'Because princes who were in line to rule empires were now waiting in line for your hand.'

'And I suppose you obliged and forgot I ever existed?'

'I couldn't quite do that, but from that moment, I began to think of you as my beloved sister. Ilavarasi! Please take me to Kandamaaran right away. Or bring him to me. I would like to know why he told such a terrible lie. Or if that is what he truly believes, I would like to dispel that misunderstanding.'

'I suppose you would like to finish off what you started in Thanjavur, then.'

'You mean ... what, exactly?'

'You didn't succeed in killing him there.'

'Kadavule! Do you think I would come to Kandamaaran's own home to kill him?'

'Why else would you choose the secret entrance?'

'There, listen carefully. The people who came to murder me are still in the next room. You can hear them walking and you can hear their voices too, can't you?'

'Why should they want to kill you?'

'They look like mantravadis. Perhaps they're from some cult that offers human sacrifices.'

'And I suppose you're quite perfect, a prince fit for the gods!' Manimeghalai said, before bursting into laughter.

'Yes, I'm quite astonished. Why should they want to catch this man with a monkey's face and an owl's stare? But after hearing what you had to say, I wonder if perhaps this was arranged by Kandamaaran. Please take me to him right away. He must either realise that he was under the wrong impression or kill me with his own hands. Why must he hire murderers? Ammani! Please call your brother right away!'

'Aiya, please don't be in such a hurry. Kandamaaran is not in town.'

'Where has he gone?'

'He has gone to Kanchi to escort Karikalar here. They will all be here by tomorrow evening. Until then, why don't you …'

'Why don't I stay here until then, you ask? That would not be right.'

'I wasn't going to ask you to stay here. The Pazhuvoor Ilaya Rani will be here in a bit. Then, not even a fly can enter this space. You must know what kind of man Pazhuvettaraiyar is. If he were to catch you here, he would have you cut to pieces. Ah! How much that old man adores his wife!' Manimeghalai said, and let out another peal of laughter.

Vandiyadevan thought back to everything that had happened the last time Pazhuvettaraiyar had come here.

'Really? Does Pazhuvettaraiyar love the Pazhuvoor Rani so very much?'

'Why, the entire land knows about his love for her! They were here some eight months ago. He would not let her out of his sight, not even to visit the antapuram! This time, they're going to be here for a few days. We've all been in a tizzy preparing an antapuram for the Pazhuvoor Rani to have all to herself. We're not sure whether she'll grace us with a darshan. Or whether the old man will permit it.'

'So, what is it you would have me do?'

'I'm trying to think ... ah! I just had an idea! There's a separate room for Kandamaaran in this palace, where he keeps his weapons. I'll take you there. Kandamaaran will be here tomorrow evening, and then you can prove your innocence—or not—to him. Just remain there until he arrives.'

'Ilavarasi! That is not right. It is most dangerous!'

'Why is it dangerous?'

'What would I say if Kandamaaran were to ask me how I got there?'

'You should tell him the truth.'

'When I told the truth, you yourself couldn't believe it. Not even with my pursuers creating a racket in the very next room!'

'Aiya! I'll investigate right away.'

'What are you going to investigate right away?'

'I'm going to go to the next room and interrogate the people there. I'll find out whether they are here to murder you, or whether they are here at your behest.'

'Aiyo! They are evil men. If you get caught with them all by yourself …'

'Who can do anything to me in my own palace? Here, see for yourself!' and with that, Manimeghalai brandished something she had tucked into her waistband, hidden from view. It was a little penknife.

'No one can come anywhere near me. And if I were to be in any danger, I have you, a hero among warriors, right here, don't I?'

'Ammani, I am unarmed at the moment.'

'Haven't you heard the saying "vallavanukku pullum aayudham"? Even a blade of grass can turn into a weapon in the hands of a truly valorous warrior. And your very name is Vallavarayar, the king of valour. Even women can fight, so long as they are armed. Why should we have any need of men then? Please don't worry. The man who was dusting the next room is a servant of our palace. He must have brought the others we can hear there. I have a feeling they're all people I know. I'll find out why they're here. Don't stand by the door. There, go and hide in that corner!'

With this, Manimeghalai strode towards the door that led into the trophy room and tried to push it open, even as Vandiyadevan rushed to the spot she had pointed out. The door in the corner led to a storeroom. But this was no ordinary storehouse for grains. There were steps inside the room. On each step, musical instruments such as the yazh, veena, madhalam and taalam had been arranged. He looked up. The steps went right up to the roof.

In the meantime, Manimeghalai had pushed open the door to the trophy room and entered. Vandiyadevan was awed by her intrepidity. At the same time, he told himself she was not in any danger.

Suddenly, the other door leading into the room opened, and Chandramati entered, calling, 'Amma! Amma!'

Vandiyadevan panicked. He slipped into the room with the musical instruments so that she wouldn't see him.

'Amma! Amma! The guests from Thanjavur have arrived! The maharani asked me to bring you there right away!' Chandramati called, and looked about the room. She made for the trophy room, the door to which was open.

If she were to stop and turn, she would be able to see Vandiyadevan. So, he climbed up a few steps. His knee struck a veena and there was a noise from the impact. Panicking, Vandiyadevan ran up a few more steps. Now, he hit his head against the roof.

But what a wonder! When his head made contact with the roof, the ceiling seemed to lift a bit. He reached his arms out and pushed at the roof. It went right up, and he could see light streaming in from the gap it created. There were sounds of a commotion from far away. And, on the other side, he could see stars shining in the sky.

Vandiyadevan's heart leapt.

He pushed the roof harder and the plank moved easily. He moved it to one side and climbed up. He tried to find his bearings. He seemed to be on one of the terraces of the palace. In fact, this was the very terrace where he had gone to sleep when he had last visited. The very spot where he had hidden behind the wide pillars and eavesdropped on the conspiracy the suzerain kings were hatching. He moved the plank back into place. It occurred to him that it was no easy task to find this particular secret escape from the roof back to the music room. But he did not have the luxury of time to reflect on and wonder at such things. He would have to find a way to escape from the palace. The goddess of luck had always been on his side. She wouldn't let him down now, surely?

Vandiyadevan looked about himself. Flags and ornate decorations were everywhere. It was a stunning sight. Adada! So this is what a royal welcome was!

Vandiyadevan walked on tiptoe, staying vigilant. The terraces were empty of people. He was in luck, he thought, and hurried on. He arrived at the very spot where he had slept the last time he had been here. From there, he could see the palace wall and the courtyard that separated the wall and the palace. The place where the kuravai koothu had been staged as well as the hall where the conspirators had gathered were visible too. But there was not a soul in sight.

The reason for this was quite obvious. There was great fanfare at the palace entrance. Hundreds of torches were being held up. The beat of drums, the sound of trumpets, the cheers of people, all rose into the air.

Everyone had gathered at the gates of the palace to welcome the Pazhuvettaraiyar brothers' entourage. Aha! There was no doubt that luck was on Vandiyadevan's side. Half a naazhigai before or after, and the terrace would not have been deserted as it was now.

He went to the vantage point from which he had seen the conspirators' gathering and peered down. No one was about. He then looked around himself again. Nobody. He looked at the wall opposite. Nob—no, wait! What was that? A face had appeared among the branches of the tree near the top of the wall! ... It looked like Azhvarkadiyaan's face ... no, chhi chhi, he was being silly. Was it a hallucination? He had imagined he had seen Azhvarkadiyaan's face back when the conspirators had conferred too. His mind was playing tricks on him.

But it was all for the best. There was no better spot to scale the wall and get out. His mind had somehow sensed it and found a way to convey it to him. He would have to escape before the crowd that had gathered to welcome the entourage came inside.

How would he climb down the wall though? Ah! Here was a way! A makeshift tent had been erected in the courtyard, perhaps for the kuravai koothu. A bamboo pole that had been fixed into the ground reached right up to the top. Vandiyadevan slid down the bamboo pole and reached the courtyard. He looked about him, ensured no one was about and was going to make a run for it when he heard a clanging noise from the terrace, where he had been moments earlier. Aha! Manimeghalai must have come looking for him. That daring woman! He was done for if she were to get hold of him again!

He ran across the open space that separated the palace from the outer wall. Once he had reached the boundary wall, he turned to look at the terrace. He could see a woman silhouetted at the spot. Was it Manimeghalai or Chandramati? He couldn't tell. But whoever she was, he owed her for keeping quiet as she had watched him run across that open space. Whoever she was, bless her. May she have a wonderful life!

Even as he silently expressed his gratitude to that woman, Vandiyadevan walked briskly along the boundary wall. He was now under the spot where he had seen Azhvarkadiyaan's face. How would he climb it though? It was incredibly high. There was no handhold or foothold on the wall.

Kadavule ... ah! There was something he could use lying right there! Some of the bamboo poles were lying in the courtyard. They must be the surplus poles, left over from when the makeshift auditorium had been erected for the kuravai koothu. He leapt to the pile and picked up one of the poles. He leaned it against the wall. It was the perfect height, reaching right to the top. He could now scale up the pole and get onto the wall. But how would he make sure it stayed in place? What if it moved as he was climbing, or slipped off the wall? Well, then he would fall down. He would have to take that risk. What was the point in doing nothing, anyway?

He tested the pole a couple of times, pressed against it and put his weight on it. It held fast. He then began to climb. When he was halfway up, the pole started slipping. Well, he was done for now. If he were to fall from this height, his bones would break. But just then, the pole stopped slipping and held steady again. It seemed a pair of hands was holding it up from the top. Was he going mad? Was this another hallucination? Well, he would know soon enough. Vandiyadevan used the pole to continue his climb.

The moment he reached the top of the wall and hoisted himself up, the pole slipped and fell to the ground. The noise it made as it crashed down sounded like a clap of thunder to his ears. Thankfully, the drumbeats from the entrance were growing louder and more intense. So no one would have heard ...

except that woman who was standing on the terrace! She would certainly have heard the pole fall. Once he had leapt onto the top of the wall, Vandiyadevan turned and looked at the terrace. Yes, the woman was still there.

For all the scares and scrapes he had encountered that evening, Vandiyadevan's audacity hadn't deserted him. He waved and saluted as if to say, 'Until next time!' at the woman, and then began to climb down the wall. It wasn't too hard to get down, because the other side of the wall wasn't smooth. There were ridges and groves. The branches of trees that grew on the road had made their way to the wall and proved useful in aiding Vandiyadevan's descent.

When he thought about how he had given Manimeghalai the slip, Vandiyadevan was quite amused at himself. He laughed. As if his laugh were echoing, he heard another laugh from another direction.

His blood ran cold. His hands trembled. He looked to see whether he could jump down the rest of the way.

A dog was waiting at the bottom, ready to spring on him.

Well, he couldn't very well climb back up. His only option was to jump down. If he did, he would have to donate at least a mouthful of flesh to the dog.

Was the sound he had just heard a human laugh? Or the bark of a dog? Was someone hiding nearby, someone who had set the dog on him?

Which was the more dangerous option: climbing back up or jumping down? Vandiyadevan couldn't make up his mind. As for his legs, they were frozen, not wanting to be preyed on by the dog who was now jumping up and down, pawing at the wall.

10

MANHUNT

Vandiyadevan wondered whether he should aim for the ground in such a manner as to evade the dog, or climb right back up the wall. He also scoured the trees nearby, trying to spot whoever might be hidden there. He thought he saw a piece of white cloth behind the foliage. It struck him that when the dog had barked, there had also been a burst of human laughter. What if someone was indeed hiding there? Was it just one man or a group? It would be a mistake to jump to the ground without knowing what he would face. He might escape from the dog, only to fall into a human trap.

When he had looked out from the terrace of the palace, he had thought he'd seen Azhvarkadiyaan's face on the boundary wall. Was it that Vaishnavite who had tired of waiting at the Ayyanaar temple and decided to set a dog on Vandiyadevan as a prank? Well, he might as well call out.

'Vaishnavare! Vaishnavare! Is this your idea of a joke?' he shouted.

Another burst of laughter came his way. But it was not Azhvarkadiyaan's voice. It seemed it would be more prudent to climb back up the wall and enter the palace again. The commotion around Periya Pazhuvettaraiyar's arrival would give him ample cover to attempt another escape. Or there was the subterranean passage. He would just have to sweet-talk Manimeghalai again and beg her forgiveness. Or he could turn to Nandini for help. She had never let him down thus far.

Vandiyadevan began to climb the wall again. The dog jumped higher and barked. Another laugh. Someone stepped out from behind the tree. The man was carrying a spear. Vandiyadevan recognised him as the Devaraalan. The Devaraalan now approached the wall.

'Appane! You've got *some* hold on life!' he said.

'And yet you come after me. Why?' Vandiyadevan asked.

'You won't get away this time!' the Devaraalan said and aimed the spear at Vandiyadevan.

For his part, Vandiyadevan was well aware of his precarious situation. How could he possibly duel from halfway up the wall with someone who was aiming a spear at him from below? And if he tried escaping his opponent by jumping, there was a hunting dog waiting for him.

'Devaraala! Careful! You have orders from your ejamaani[1], the Pazhuvoor Rani. She told you all not to harm me, remember?'

The Devaraalan shrieked with laughter and said, 'The Pazhuvoor Rani is not my ejamaani! No rani of any kingdom is my ejaamani! It is only Bhadrakali Durga Parameshwari who can call herself my ejamaani.'

'Why, Durga Parameshwari is my clan deity. It is her grace that allowed me to escape from a burning ship in the middle of the ocean. If you lay a finger on me, Durga Parameshwari will turn you to ashes!' Vandiyadevan said.

'If you're truly a devotee of Durga, you must do something for me. That's the only way I'll spare your life.'

'What do you want me to do? First, ask your dog to move away.'

'A Veera Vaishnavite came this way. If you help me catch him, I'll spare you.'

'Why do you want to catch him?' Vandiyadevan asked.

'I have vowed to offer a Vaishnavite as a sacrifice to the goddess, that's why,' the Devaraalan said.

At this point, the creeper to which Vandiyadevan was clinging for balance began to peel off the wall. Vandiyadevan strategised. Was there a way he could land on the Devaraalan's neck without getting impaled by the spear?

'That Veera Vaishnavite is my dear friend!' he called. 'Why don't you offer me as a sacrifice in his stead?'

'In that case, sacrifice yourself to this spear right away!' the Devaraalan called and aimed his spear.

Vandiyadevan let go of the creeper and aimed for a point on the ground from which he could grab the spear from the Devaraalan's hands. The speed of his fall sent him rolling. The Devaraalan watched in shock. Then, he recovered and aimed his spear again.

Just then, a figure came running from behind the Devaraalan and hit him on the head with a stick. The Devaraalan collapsed on Vandiyadevan.

The dog leapt on the attacker, but Azhvarkadiyaan was prepared for this assault too. He spread out the cloth he'd worn over his shoulders and threw it over the dog's head. This disoriented the dog, who couldn't see a thing with the cloth thrown over his head. In those precious seconds, the Vaishnavite improvised a lasso with a strong vine he had brought from the forest, and threw it around the dog's neck. He went on to tie the animal to a tree.

In the meantime, Vandiyadevan had pushed the Devaraalan off himself and got up. One whack from the Vaishnavite was all it had taken to render the man unconscious. Vandiyadevan and Azhvarkadiyaan collected more vines, which they used to bind the Devaraalan's hands and feet. Vandiyadevan helped himself to the spear, while Azhvarkadiyaan kept his stick handy.

Except at the entrance, the palace of Sambuvarayar was surrounded by forest. If the two men wandered far, they might have got lost. So, they stuck to the boundary wall as they hurried on.

'I thought you were clever and resourceful,' Azhvarkadiyaan panted, as they walked. 'I realise I was wrong.'

'Are you talking about my rushing into the secret passage? Do you know what terrible secrets I have unearthed because of that foray?' Vandiyadevan said.

'That's as may be. But when the Devaraalan asked if you would help him catch the Vaishnavite, why didn't you just say yes, instead of putting yourself in peril?' Vandiyadevan asked.

'It's all thanks to the company I keep,' Vandiyadevan said.

'Whose company are you talking about? I don't think I've ever taught you to make such a grievous error?'

'I'm not talking about you, aiya. I meant Ponniyin Selvar. Having met him and been around him, I'm not able to bring myself to lie.'

'Not even to save your own life? So you're a champion of truth now?'

'Not just that. I knew you must be hiding somewhere nearby. If you'd heard me promise the Devaraalan I would help catch you and taken me at my word, was it likely you'd have come forward to help me as you just did?'

'Appane! You're quite brilliant. There's no doubt. To be honest, I was waiting with bated breath to hear how you would respond to the Devaraalan's question.'

'See? I was right in thinking you're obsessively suspicious of everyone and everything. That aside, I would never betray a friend, even in word. But, tell me, you promised to wait by the Ayyanaar temple. How did you end up here? If I'd used the subterranean passage to get out and you hadn't been waiting there, I'd have been in a soup!' Vandiyadevan said.

'There wasn't much chance of your getting out alive through that passage. Not long after you went in, the conspirators entered it. Since you're resourceful, I figured you'd find another way to get out. It was most likely you'd climb the wall to escape, I thought.'

'Is that why you came here?'

'Not that alone. The conspirators left the Devaraalan to stand guard while the rest went in. They would have to be sure the Ayyanaar temple was deserted when they returned. They must have made some sort of sign to him. But I didn't realise that. I thought everyone had gone inside. I was also worried you'd be trapped there all alone. Besides, I wanted to figure out how one opened the secret passage from outside. So, I went near the sacrificial slab and was trying to open it. Then, I heard the sound of footsteps behind me and turned. The Devaraalan was coming that way, spear in hand. Remember, the conspirators had said long ago that they would kill me on sight? I was unarmed. So all I could do was run for my life. Because it was such a dense forest, he wasn't able to catch me. After a while, it seemed he had given up the chase.

'I figured it would be safe to leave the forest and use the Rajpath. I saw a hut some distance away. There was a little lamp in the doorway. I decided to go there and ask the way to the Rajpath. I observed it from some distance away. That turned out to be a very good thing. The Devaraalan was standing at the door of the hut. A girl and a dog were nearby. The Devaraalan said something to the girl and then set off with the dog. The dog turned towards the direction in which I was hiding and barked. So I knew I was in greater danger than ever. I dispelled the notion of getting onto the main road and ran back into the forest. The dog's barks gave me some idea of where they were headed. Even as I was running, my mind made its calculations. It would be impossible to run around the forest and hide all night. They would find a way to trap me. I would be hard put to take on the Devaraalan's spear and the dog's jaws at the same time.

'Just as I was thinking about all this, I spotted the walls of this palace. I figured if I could climb the wall and get into the palace, I'd be able to find an escape. I had just reached the top of the wall when I saw you running across the terraces. I realised your plan involved jumping over the wall, so I got back down.

The two of us together could take on the Devaraalan and his dog. I was quite confident of this. I heard the dog barking very close to me, so I scaled a tree quickly. The Devaraalan and the dog approached the very tree I had climbed. Before he could find me, he must have seen you trying to scale down the wall. He made for the spot where you would land, along with the dog. Well, you know what happened from that point.'

'Vaishnavare! What is your opinion on the power of destiny?'

'What a question! What made you think of destiny all of a sudden?'

'They say Brahma writes out the destiny of each person even as one is born. Do you believe this?'

'No, I don't. I don't believe in destiny. If one were to put all faith in one's destiny, it would make no sense to believe that one can attain the lotus feet of Lord Vishnu through devotion and service, does it? Do you know what the Azhvars say? They say …'

'Let the Azhvars say whatever they want. But I have become a complete believer in destiny. I think everything unfolds according to one's fate. If that were not the case, I would not have been able to make my escape today.'

'Appane! It wasn't your destiny, but your decisions that saved you.'

'Not at all. My decisions landed me in great danger, and destiny got me out of it.'

By this time, they had reached the end of the forest. They could see the entrance to the palace from there. It was evident that there was great commotion. Pazhuvettaraiyar's entourage, complete with his elephant and horses and infantry, was approaching the palace gates. The palace had been decorated in opulent fashion. Sambuvarayar was waiting with a welcoming committee to receive his guests. Hundreds of torches had been lit, making the night bright as day. Drums, trumpets, thaarai, thappattai and all sorts of other instruments were playing.

Azhvarkadiyaan grabbed Vandiyadevan's hand and said, 'Come, let's go! Someone might catch sight of us.'

'No one's going to so much as glance this side. Even if someone does, my destiny will save me. Don't you want to see the grand sight of Periya Pazhuvettaraiyar stepping off his elephant?'

'Is that all you're waiting for?'

'I'd like to see if the Pazhuvoor Rani Nandini is riding with him on the elephant or has chosen to arrive in her palanquin.'

'Thambi! Don't trust that destiny will always be on your side. It could take the form of a mayamohini and be your undoing too.'

'I'm not the kind to be entranced quite so easily, Vaishnavare! That is the destiny of others.'

An elephant arrived at the palace gate and stood regally. Periya Pazhuvettaraiyar got down from his ride, followed by the Pazhuvoor Ilaiya Rani.

'Oh, so the Pazhuvoor Ilaiya Rani did not come in the palanquin. He has brought her along with him, for all the world to see,' Azhvarkadiyaan said.

'That's all I wanted to know. We can leave now,' Vandiyadevan said and retreated.

But Azhvarkadiyaan was in no hurry to leave. He stood where he was, staring at the Pazhuvoor Ilaiya Rani. Either by coincidence or because she had felt his gaze, Nandini turned and glanced in their direction.

She noticed Azhvarkadiyaan's face peeping out from the darkness of the trees. Suddenly, a frightened expression took over her face. Periya Pazhuvettaraiyar noticed the change in his wife's countenance and looked in the same direction as her. He noticed two figures standing among the trees. He spoke into Sambuvarayar's ear, and the latter signalled to two of his soldiers and gave them orders.

The musical instruments blared their welcome, and Pazhuvettaraiyar and his Ilaiya Rani entered the palace.

At the same time, two horsemen entered the forest near the walls of the palace. They were hard put to lead the horses through the undergrowth. They went a fair distance without finding anyone. They had gone through almost the entire forest and were about to emerge onto the fields on the other side.

'Anna! There doesn't appear to be anyone in the forest. The old man is hallucinating,' one of them said.

At this point, a dog howled.

'Thambi! Do you know when dogs howl?' the other one asked.

'When someone dies,' the first one said.

'They also howl when they see ghosts and ghouls and betaals and so on,' the second said.

'Perhaps it took you for a ghost?'

'No, thambi, it took you for a ghoul.'

Just then, they heard unearthly laughter from somewhere over their heads. Startled, both men looked up. There were two betaals, sitting on a tree over their heads. Each of the betaals slapped one of the soldiers across the face, caught his neck and threw him off his horse. Then, with both soldiers on the ground and both horses at their command, the betaals crossed the forest and headed for the fields.

11

FRIEND? OR FOE?

Aditya Karikalan, with his entourage and escort, was nearing the scenic spot where the Manimuthar river joined the Vellaaru. They spoke about the reception the prince had received at Tirumudukundram the previous night and the work that was being done at the temple in that town.

'I can't stop thinking about what Sundaramurti Nayanar did at Tirumudukundram! I love it!' Parthibendran said.

'What are you referring to?' Aditya Karikalan asked.

'His refusal to sing in praise of old people.'

'I have no idea what you're talking about. You'll have to explain.'

Parthibendran narrated the story.

Once, when Sundaramurti Nayanar was on a pilgrimage, he visited Tirumudukundram, also known as Vriddhachalam. He made straight for the Shiva temple, as was his wont. The temple priests led him to the sanctum sanctorum and, once he had prayed, requested him to grace the temple with a padigam in praise of the deity.

'Let's see … what is the name of the temple deity?' Sundaramurti asked.

They had named the deity after 'Tirumudukundram', which meant 'revered old mountain', sanskritising it to 'Vriddhagiriswarar'—lord of the old mountain.

Sundaramurti made a face. Did he have to compose a padigam in praise of an old man now?

'All right, what is Amman's name?' he asked, referring to the consort of the deity.

'Vriddhagiriswari.'

'You've given the lord the title of "old man". But couldn't you have spared his wife at least? I'm not going to sing in praise of an old couple!' Sundaramurti said and stormed out of the temple.

The priests knew that the prestige of having Sundaramurti Nayanar compose a padigam in praise of their town temple was no small matter. They did not want the temple to be left out. They hastily consecrated another idol of the consort and named her 'Balambika'. Then, they sought out Sundaramurti, who was in another town by the time, and explained that they had made amends. They implored him to return to their town and sing of the temple. Sundaramurti obliged and composed a padigam at the temple in praise of Balambika and Vriddhagiriswarar.

When Aditya Karikalan heard the story, he shook with laughter.

'Perhaps a visiting poet came up with the same objection as Sundaramurti when he arrived at the Pazhuvoor palace, refusing to sing in praise of an old couple. Perhaps that's why the old man married Nandini?' he said.

That made Parthibendran and Kandamaaran roll over with laughter. They nearly fell off their horses as they held their sides.

Once they had spent themselves, Parthibendran said, 'I wonder why God created such a thing as ageing. Why can't we live out our years looking the same and then die?'

'Why does it matter whether God created ageing or not? It is up to us whether we age, isn't it?' Aditya Karikalan said.

'How?' Kandamaaran asked.

'Do we see Abhimanyu and Aravan as old men?' Aditya Karikalan asked.

His friends fell silent.

'At the chitra mandapam of the Thanjavur Palace, you'll find portraits of my ancestors. Vijayalaya Chozhar, Aditya Chozhar, Parantaka Chakravarti are all seen as elderly kings. But my great-uncle Rajadityar … have you seen his portrait? He is forever young, a strapping warrior standing tall and bursting with the vigour of youth! Which of us will be as lucky, I wonder …'

The other two did not like the turn the conversation was taking. They remained silent.

'Why have you fallen silent? Why are you so scared of death? We'll discard this body for a new one. Why fear death? If my friend Vandiyadevan were here, he would agree. It's not easy to find a man as dynamic as he. You could take him to the gates of Yamalokam and he would remain cheerful, laughing and joking as always,' Aditya Karikalan said.

Just then, they were distracted by clouds of dust. Two horses were galloping towards them from far away. The horsemen were upon them in the blink of an eye. They were going so fast, it appeared they would go past the entourage without so much as noticing that it was Aditya Karikalan's.

Kandamaaran and Parthibendran readied their spears to stop the men from crossing. Who dared display such arrogance?

However, before they could cross their spears and block the path, the horsemen reined in their rides.

Vandiyadevan and Azhvarkadiyaan jumped off the horses.

Aditya Karikalan couldn't contain his excitement upon seeing his friend. He jumped off his horse too and ran to welcome him with a warm embrace.

'Thambi, you'll live a hundred years!' he said. 'I was just speaking of you!'

The envy this vignette stoked in Kandamaaran and Parthibendran was evident on their faces. They led their horses a few steps further and stopped. They noticed more horses approaching. It wasn't long before the other riders had arrived. Kandamaaran recognised them as employees of the Kadambur palace. He went to confer with them, and then trotted up to Aditya Karikalan.

'Komagane![1] This man is a friend of yours and was a friend of mine too. But I'm afraid I must charge him with a crime. He is a traitor, a snehadrohi, not a friend but a foe! He stabbed me in the back and wounded me badly. So, it is my duty to warn you to be on your guard around him,' Kandamaaran said.

12

WHEN THE SPEAR BROKE

When Aditya Karikalan heard the charge Kandamaaran had brought against his dear friend Vandiyadevan, he almost collapsed with laughter.

'Kandamaara! Vandiyadevan stabbed you in the back, did he? Why did you turn your back to him then?' he said, and began to laugh again.

Kandamaaran's dusky countenance turned red. His eyes turned into scarlet gourds and his lips trembled.

'Aiya! Do you consider this a laughing matter?' he asked.

'Kandamaara! You say I shouldn't laugh? Laughter is God's gift to mankind, denied to cows and goats and horses and lions ... even to monkeys, which are so fond of pranks. Man has a monopoly on laughter. And you ask me not to laugh? It's been a very long time since I laughed. My friend! The sound of my laughter has surprised even me. And you tell me not to laugh?' Aditya Karikalan asked.

'Aiya! I would rejoice if you laughed in joy. But please don't laugh at the idea of my fleeing from this great warrior. He attacked me from behind when I wasn't expecting such an ambush. It was thanks to the grace of Durga Devi and the care of Nandini Devi that I survived. You must conduct an investigation into the treacherous act he committed and make sure justice is done. Or grant me the authority to punish him myself!' Kandamaaran said.

'My friend! I will investigate this myself and ensure justice is done. It has never been said that a man who asked a king of the Sembiyan clan for justice walked away without seeing it done. The preceptor of our dynasty, Sibi, sliced off his own flesh in chunks to ensure that justice was served to a dove. Manuneethi Chozhan sacrificed the life of his own son to assuage the hurt of a cow who had lost her calf to his chariot. You are not less deserving than a dove and a cow. I will not deny you justice. But please be patient until I'm done interrogating him. Vallavaraya! Before you recount the details of your journey, it would be best if you responded to Kandamaaran's charge against you. What is your claim? Is it true that you stabbed him in the back? In that case, what led you to stoop so low? To carry out such a cowardly act? What was your motive?'

'Ilavarase! I did not stab this great war hero with a spear, not from the front and not from the back. I did not sit in hiding, waiting for him to appear so

I could stab him. He was lying in a pool of blood, having been stabbed in the back. I carried him on my shoulders to Senthan Amudan's home so that he would be saved. But now I regret saving his life. I wish I had pierced him in the chest and finished him off. Because I have failed to fulfil my duty to my liege out of loyalty to my friend. Aiya, he said I was no friend, but a foe. He called me a "snehadrohi". But he is not just a snehadrohi but an ejamaanadrohi himself, a traitor to his lord. Ask him where and under what circumstances he was stabbed in the back! Ask him whom he was escorting into Pazhuvettaraiyar's palace through a secret passage! Ask him whom he met in the secret treasury of Periya Pazhuvettaraiyar that night! Ask him what happened on the day of the first flood during the month of Aadi, at his palace in Kadambur! Ask him who was hiding in the closed palanquin that arrived at his palace that day!'

Kandamaaran, quivering all over, his tongue rolling on itself, cried, 'Ade! You scum! Stop blabbering! Or you'll be fodder for my spear!'

He held his spear aloft.

Aditya Karikalan was taken aback by Kandamaaran's tantrum.

He reached for the spear and bent the shaft with his iron hands. The spear broke in two. Aditya Karikalan tossed the pieces far away and said, 'Careful! I can't sit back and watch my friends fighting before my eyes. Parthibendra! If either one of them so much as reaches for his sword or spear, it is your duty to arrest the offender right away.'

At this, Vandiyadevan handed over his sword to Parthibendran, who received it with reluctance.

'Kandamaara! Vallavarayan has responded to your accusation. I will do my due diligence and give my verdict. Are you going to answer his questions?' Aditya Karikalan asked.

Kandamaaran stumbled and stuttered and slurred as he said, 'Aiya! I have taken an oath not to speak about those matters to anyone.'

Parthibendran intervened now and said, 'Arase! The charges these two are bringing against each other seem to have to do with some woman. It would be best to question them separately.'

'True, Parthiba, I share your opinion. The three of you have met the Pazhuvoor Ilaiya Rani separately, and have fallen into her trap. You're all besotted, and that's why you're trying to undermine each other,' Aditya Karikalan said, before roaring with laughter.

Parthibendran contorted his face and said, 'Prabhu! You appear to have decided to laugh away every matter of importance today. I might as well tell you what I have to say. I too have my suspicions about Vandiyadevan. I'll tell you the most important one now. Your beloved brother jumped into the stormy seas in order to save this man from a burning ship. That was the last time Ponniyin Selvar was seen. And now, Vandiyadevan shows up alone and unharmed!

Ask him what became of your brother. If he has indeed drowned at sea, it is this man who is to blame for it!'

'How would you like to respond to this?' Aditya Karikalan now asked Vandiyadevan.

'Aiya! Before I respond to his questions, I would like him to answer one of mine. It was he who left from Lanka with Ponniyin Selvar on his ship. Prime Minister Aniruddhar and Senapati Boothi Vikrama Kesari beseeched him to remain in Lanka. And yet, the prince chose to follow his elder brother's orders and boarded the ship that was to bring him to you. Why did Parthibendran not ensure that he handed him over safely to you? Why did he stand there watching as Ponniyin Selvar dove into the sea? Why didn't he stop the prince? Ponniyin Selvar risked his life to save a poor orphan, but this Pallava scion and his men didn't think to risk their lives to save the prince, did they? They just stood there as if they were watching a show when the waves swallowed Ponniyin Selvar, didn't they?'

Parthibendran was fuming. His face was red, his hands shook, his lips trembled, his body twitched. 'Aiya! This fool seems to be accusing me. He might even say I killed the prince with my own hands. I cannot brook this for a moment!'

Aditya Karikalan stared at him and said, 'Parthiba! It is as I said. The three of you, my dearest friends, have reached a stage where you're happy to tear each other to pieces. I don't blame you for this. I have learnt that the Pazhuvoor Rani's powers are such. I want you and Kandamaaran to ride some distance ahead. I will ride with Vandiyadevan and learn the details of his journey. I will also interrogate him and get to the bottom of the accusations the two of you have levied against him. But know this for certain. The strong friendship between the three of you must be restored. Nothing would cause me more distress than infighting among you.'

Kandamaaran and Parthibendran had no choice but to ride ahead.

Azhvarkadiyaan came up to Vandiyadevan now and whispered into his ear, 'Appane! You've got quite clever! You haven't lied and you haven't given away the truth, and you've handled it all very well, got out of a situation rather strategically, eh?'

It was only now that Aditya Karikalan noticed Azhvarkadiyaan.

'Oho! Who is this now? I have seen you somewhere, sometime ...' he said.

'Yes, arase. It was some years ago.'

'Your voice is familiar too.'

'True, aiya. Three years ago, you heard my voice at a critical point.'

Suddenly, a shadow crossed over Aditya Karikalan's countenance. 'Three years ago ... a critical point ... what was it? Was this a voice I heard when I was on the banks of the Vaigai river, searching for my enemy? Could it be that voice?'

'Indeed, it was my voice, arase! It was I who told you your enemy's hideout, from my own hiding spot in a tree.'

'Aha! What a terrible day that was! My body trembles at the memory of the frenzied rage that had taken over me that day. Vaishnavane! Why were you hiding in the forest that day? Why did you choose to be a disembodied voice?'

'Arase! You yourself spoke of the frenzied rage that had taken over you that day. You were cutting down anyone who crossed your path. I wished to live a little longer ...'

'Was that the only reason? I shouted until I was hoarse that day, calling, "Let the disembodied voice manifest itself and show me the way!" And yet you would not come out of hiding.'

'The sister I raised ... who is now the Pazhuvoor Ilaiya Rani ... I did not wish to face her wrath.'

'And yet, you decided that it would be all right for me alone to face her wrath! Ada sandaala!' Aditya Karikalan said, running a hand over the dagger tucked into his waistband.

Vandiyadevan panicked. It seemed Azhvarkadiyaan's life would end that day.

He said, as gently as he could, 'Aiya ... this Vaishnavite bears a message from the prime minister. Please hear him out before you punish him.'

'Aha! What would be the point of punishing him? Or anyone else?' Aditya Karikalan said.

Azhvarkadiyaan seemed quite undaunted by Aditya Karikalan's anger. With a bizarre smile on his face, he said, 'Arase! I didn't meet you face to face all this time because I knew I would be subjected to your rage. My sister's wrath hasn't subsided either. She has refused to meet me in spite of every attempt I have made. But her anger against you seems to have dissipated. It is after reading her affectionate letter that you started for Kadambur, isn't it?'

'Aha! And how did you know this?' Aditya Karikalan asked.

'Aiya! I serve the prime minister. Nothing happens in Chozha Naadu without the prime minister learning of it,' Azhvarkadiyaan said.

'You just wait and watch … one day, I'm going to banish both that Anbil Aniruddhan and you! Now, get on your horse. I'd like you and Vandiyadevan to ride on either side of me. We'll talk on the way.'

13

MANIMEGHALAI'S SECRET

Nandini was reclining against the ornate bed that had been arranged for her in the specially decorated antapuram of the guest quarters at the Kadambur Palace. She had ornamented herself particularly well that day, and glowed with an ethereal beauty. Her half-closed eyes revealed that she was daydreaming. Every time her kohled eyelids fluttered open, her magnetic eyes seemed to flash lightning-like beams of thought. Although she appeared to be half-asleep, it was evident that her mind was active as ever.

A keen observer might notice that her eyes were constantly drifting towards the plumes of smoke emanating from the incense burner in a corner of the room. The smoke spiralled upwards, dissipating into thin air. What visions did Nandini see in the smoke? She sighed heavily, all of a sudden. Her coral lips mouthed the words in a whisper: 'True, true, my dreams have dissipated like those spirals of smoke. At least the incense leaves behind a delightful fragrance when it disappears. My dreams have left only sorrow and pain and suffering and calumny and disgrace behind …'

'Devi! Devi! May I come in?'

It was Manimeghalai's soft voice.

'Come, amma, come … why would you ask me permission to enter a room in your own home?' Nandini asked.

Manimeghalai entered the room and walked towards Nandini with deliberation. But there was such eagerness in her face and enthusiasm in her gait that she might as well have been singing and dancing her way towards the Pazhuvoor Rani.

Nandini sat up and gestured for Manimeghalai to sit on the ivory chair by the bed.

Manimeghalai sat down and said, 'Devi! My brother has told me how I must conduct myself around you. He has spoken to me at length about the propriety and manners of the people from the southern regions. He said I must never enter a room without asking permission.'

'Let the people of the southern regions and their propriety and manners run to ruin! Forget everything your brother has taught you right away. And stop calling me "Devi" and "Maharani". Call me "Akka"!'

'Akka! Akka! It won't bother you if I keep coming to you and badgering you, will it?'

'It *will* bother me if you keep coming to me and badgering me. The only way we can avoid that is for you to stay right here with me and not go away,' Nandini said, with a warm smile.

Manimeghalai was entranced by the smile. She stared at Nandini's face for a bit and then said, 'I have never seen such a beauty as you, not even in portraits!'

'Penne! You also don't go and fall in love with me! I'm already being called a "mayamohini" by the people of this land. They say I bewitch every man who meets me.'

'Akka! If such calumny were to fall on my ears, I would slice off the tongue of the person who speaks it before I do anything else!' Manimeghalai said.

'There's no point in blaming wagging tongues, Manimeghalai. I have married an old man, haven't I? It is natural for people to say such things.'

Manimeghalai frowned. 'Yes, yes, the thought upsets me. My brother laments it too. But that doesn't mean one can cast aspersions on someone over a personal choice ...'

'Let them talk if they want to, Manimeghalai. Sita Devi herself was not exempt from being the subject of gossip. What did Sita lose over that? All right, let's not talk of me anymore. Tell me about yourself!'

'What do I have to say about myself, akka?'

'Adi, kalli! You promised to tell me a secret this evening, didn't you? And now you ask me what you have to say?' Nandini said, and pinched Manimeghalai's cheek affectionately.

'Akka! I want to be by your side forever. If they were to organise a swayamvaram for me and allow women to marry each other, I would throw the garland around your neck,' Manimeghalai said.

'It hasn't even been a whole day since you met me. And yet here you are, seducing me with speech, making a poet's promises! I'm quite happy to hear all this though. I've often longed for a dear friend and missed having a sakhi, and now here you are. The women of all the royal households in Chozha Naadu, the girls of the suzerain kings' families, seek out that Pazhaiyarai pisaasu. But at least you've stayed back for me. What you said sometime ago, though, can never happen. There has never been an instance of a woman marrying a woman. You will have to end up marrying some man or the other ...'

'What if I choose to remain a maiden forever?'

'No, kanne, that isn't possible. This world will never allow you to remain a maiden. Your parents will not allow it, and neither will your brother. Their hearts will know no rest until they string you around some man's neck. All right, so tell me ... if you must absolutely marry, whom would you like to spend the rest of your life with, tell me?'

'Tell me my options, akka, and I'll answer you.'

'All right, all right, I'll do that. Would you like to marry the symbol of Shiva bhakti, Madurantaka

Devar? Or the war hero and lion of the battlefield, Aditya Karikalar?'

Suddenly, Manimeghalai threw her head back and laughed, as if she had just thought of something funny.

'Why do you laugh, Manimeghalai? Do you think I'm joking? Your brother has invited me here for the express purpose of discussing this matter. Aditya Karikalar will be here soon, as will your brother. I have promised to find out what is in your heart and tell him,' Nandini said.

'But I myself don't know what is in my heart, akka. What do I do?'

'Well, at least tell me why you laughed.'

'When you spoke Madurantakar's name, something came to my mind. He had visited this palace four months ago. He arrived in your closed palanquin, with the curtains down, so that no one saw him. We women of the antapuram did not know this. We thought it was you who had arrived in the palanquin. We were wondering why the Pazhuvoor Rani had not come to the antapuram. Akka! You said it would not be possible for women to marry each other, didn't you? Marrying Madurantakar would be quite like marrying a woman!'

Nandini smiled and said, 'Yes, I was quite sure you wouldn't want to marry Madurantakar. I told your brother as much. Besides, Madurantakar is already married to my brother-in-law's daughter. She is demanding and arrogant. You will not last a day as her co-wife. So, am I to understand that you have lost your heart to Prince Aditya Karikalar?'

'I would not say that either, akka. I have never set eyes on him. How could I possibly lose my heart to him?'

'Adiye! Have royal women ever had the opportunity to set eyes on a match before they lose their hearts to a husband? Haven't you read in the epics and heard in stories of women who fall in love by looking at portraits and listening to the feats of men?'

'Yes, I have. And I am also aware that Aditya Karikalar is an intrepid warrior whose fame has spread throughout the world. Akka! I believe Aditya Karikalar chopped off Veerapandiyan's head with one stroke of his blade. Is that true?'

Manimeghalai did not notice how Nandini's face transformed at her words. She did not see the Pazhuvoor Rani's fearsome expression, since the latter kept her face turned away until her features had settled into their usual aspect, the old loveliness that entranced everyone who saw her.

'Manimeghalai! Do you think it is a heroic feat to lop off someone's head in one stroke? Isn't it a demonic act?'

'I don't understand, akka. Isn't it a heroic deed to vanquish one's enemy? How would that qualify as demonic?'

'Well, think about this. Let us say someone you love very much ... your brother, for instance, or perhaps a beloved whom you intend to marry ... let us say an enemy is marching towards this man, intending to chop off his head. This man who means the world to you is wounded and confined to bed, and his enemy is marching towards him, swinging his sword. Would you call this enemy heroic?'

Manimeghalai contemplated this for some time and then said, 'Akka! You have put a strange question to me. But I'll tell you what I think. If I were to find myself in that situation, I would not be a mute witness to it. I would snatch the sword from the enemy and kill him with his own blade!'

Nandini pulled Manimeghalai into an embrace and said, 'My kanne! What a response! I worry that such an intelligent woman as you might never find a husband who deserves her. I doubt that even Aditya Karikalar merits your hand in marriage.'

'I agree with you, akka. Having heard accounts of Karikalar's character, I find myself rather afraid of him. Shall I tell you my secret, shall I tell you something I've been holding within my heart?' Manimeghalai asked.

14

WILL THE DREAM COME TRUE?

Nandini cupped Manimeghalai's chin and searched her lovely eyes.

'My kanmani! It's best you keep your secret to yourself. It hasn't even been a day since we first met. You should only let your oldest friends in on matters of the heart.'

'No, akka. With you, I have the sense of being around an old friend. My heart wants to confide in you, tell you things I have told no one else. And I have the courage to ask you things I haven't dared ask anyone else.'

'Then please do, kanne!'

'They speak of illusions in stories, of someone appearing before us without actually being there. Is that really possible, akka? Can such a thing happen?'

'At times. People whom we love dearly, perhaps more than we should, we can sometimes see them even when they're not really there. Why, you must have heard the story of Mayakannan[1] surely, Manimeghalai? And seen plays staged about the episode? Kamsa was obsessed with his nephew Krishna. And so, he would see the boy everywhere he looked, even when Krishna was not really there. He would aim knives at these visions, only for them to fall on the floor or bounce off the walls. And then, there were gopikas who were in love with Krishna. They too would see him everywhere. They would run to hug pillars and trees, and even the running waters of the river, thinking they saw their beloved Krishna there. Adiye, Manimeghalai, who is the mayakannan who has caught your fancy?'

'Akka! I first saw him in person only four months ago. Before that, my brother Kandamaaran would speak of him often. But I never saw an image of him in my mind's eye. It was only after I met him that he began to appear in my dreams. At times, even during the day, I would think I saw him somewhere ...'

'And you saw that mayavi yesterday too, didn't you?'

'Yes, akka. How did you know?'

'Has no one told you about my magical powers?'

'They have. But is that true, akka?'

'Why don't you put me to the test? Would you like me to use my magical powers to divine the identity of the young man who has captured your heart?'

'Please do. Let's see. The thing is ... I can't bring myself to speak his name,' Manimeghalai said, blushing.

Nandini closed her eyes for some time and then opened them.

'The man who has captivated you is the scion of the Vaanar clan, Vallavarayan Vandiyadevan. Am I right?'

'Akka! It is certainly true that you possess magical powers!'

'Adi penne! When you're so in love with someone, why haven't you told your brother about it? Why tempt Madurantakar? Why try to persuade Aditya Karikalar? And why drag me all the way here?'

'Akka! My brother Kandamaaran does not like him ...'

'Why does that matter? Is your brother going to marry him? But ... didn't you say it was your brother who spoke of him to you? And that it was your brother who invited him here?'

'Yes, it was Kandamaaran who told me about him and who brought him to the antapuram too. But he had a change of heart later. And not without reason. I believe he stabbed my brother in Thanjavur, akka! It seems my brother recuperated from the wound in your palace? And it was your tender care that saved his life?'

'Your brother has exaggerated my role in this. But let's leave that aside. What are you going to do now? Your beloved has made an enemy of your brother.'

'But do you know what he says?'

'Who is "he"?'

'He is ... him! The person whose name you spoke sometime ago. He swears he did not stab Kandamaaran. Someone else had stabbed my brother and left him to die. And it was *he* who saved Kandamaaran.'

'And when did he tell you this?'

'Yesterday.'

'So, you saw Vandiyadevan in person yesterday? You said you had an illusion that he was there?'

'That's the thing, akka, I'm all confused. I don't know whether it was really he that I saw, or whether it was an illusion. When I think back to the events of yesterday, I get the sense that it was all a dream. Akka! They say the spirits of the dead can come back and talk to us. Is that true?'

Manimeghalai's voice was laced with terror as she asked the question. Nandini's entire body shook and her eyes darted about as she said, 'Yes, it is! People who die young, who go before their time, their spirits appear before the living. If it is someone who has been beheaded, sometimes the head appears alone, and sometimes the headless body appears. At times, both appear side by side and ask, "Have you avenged my death?"' With this, she turned to Manimeghalai and asked, 'Adi penne! Why did you ask me this question? Are you afraid your beloved has met such a fate? Who aroused such a suspicion in your heart?'

'There is a man in this palace who is a medium of sorts. I had sent for him. I believe someone beat him up yesterday. His wife, the Devaraatti, came and told me.'

'Chhi, chhi! Don't believe all this!'

'I didn't believe her. A spirit cannot be touched, can it, akka?'

'A spirit cannot be touched, and neither can an illusion. Why did you ask? Did you reach out and touch the man who has claimed your heart?'

'That's what I'm all confused about. I feel as if I did touch him. But then, when I think of some other things, I am not sure.'

'Tell me exactly what transpired yesterday, and then I can allay your suspicions.'

'As you say, akka! If I get incoherent and go back and forth, stop me and ask whatever questions you want to,' Manimeghalai said. 'Yesterday, at around this very time, I was in this room. I was here to follow my brother's instructions and ensure that the maids had provided every comfort for your stay. Then, I saw the mirror here and was looking at my reflection ...'

'Admiring your own beauty, I presume.'

'Nothing of the sort, akka. Don't I know just how I look?'

'Why, what's wrong with how you look? Won't Rathi and Indrani and Menaka and Urvashi envy your looks?'

'All of them put together cannot compete with the dust on your feet, akka!'

'All right, all right, that's enough. Now, go on. You were looking at your reflection ...'

'And all of a sudden, another face appeared next to mine in the mirror.'

'Your beloved's face?'

'Yes. I jumped out of my skin.'

'Why? You said you've often seen his face in your dreams.'

'But this was a bit different. He would appear some distance away in my dreams. Even in those illusions during the day, he would be far away. But yesterday … he … it was as if he was coming up from behind me to … I'm … I'm not able to go on …'

Manimeghalai was blushing.

'Oh, do tell, kalli!'

'It was … it was as if he was coming from behind to kiss me on the cheek. I turned back in shock. But there was no one there. Then, I could not see him in the mirror either. And then something struck me. I showed you the secret door that opens out into the trophy hall, no? Yesterday, the mirror had been kept right across from the door. I thought perhaps someone had opened that door and was peeping in from the trophy room. But then I realised it was not possible. How could a stranger have come to the trophy room? Even so, I decided to make sure, and so I opened the door and went into the trophy room.'

Nandini was sitting up, listening intently. 'So, was the thief hiding in the trophy room? Did he get caught?'

'What is this, akka, you called him a "thief"?'

'I was referring to his having stolen your heart, my dear. Was he in the trophy room?'

'That's what bewilders me, akka! He wasn't there. Instead, I found our servant dusting the room. That man, Idumbankaari, has a face is exactly like that of the statue outside the Ayyanaar temple, of the Kaaduvetti Karuppan. I asked him if anyone else had come to the room, and he said no.'

'Do you think he was lying?'

'I don't know. But I had the sense that someone else was hiding there. I decided to let things unfold by themselves and came back here.'

'Did things unfold, then?'

'Hold on, I'm coming to that! Once I closed the door, I decided to listen for voices in the trophy room. And sure enough, I heard them! I was wondering what I should do next when *this* door here opened. I hid the lamp and waited in the dark. There is a little round door within the main door. And someone was trying to enter the room from there. This person said, "Abayam! Abayam! I'm in danger, please show me compassion and save me!" The voice and physique seemed to be his, so I helped him inside and then brought out the lamp to see his face. It was indeed he.'

'Manimeghalai! What a magical story this is! It's like something from the Vikram-Betal folk tales!'

'And it's not over. When I saw the man I had been dreaming about for four months in person, my heart leapt. My body tingled. But I made a show of anger when I spoke to him. How dare he enter the women's quarters, I demanded. He said a group of men was chasing him to kill him. I mocked him for being a coward. He explained that he was unarmed.

Then, I asked him why he had stabbed my brother. He swore he hadn't, akka!'

'And I suppose you believed him!'

'At the time, his explanation seemed believable. But when I think of everything that happened after, I'm not sure what to believe.'

'And what happened after?'

'Even as I was speaking to him, I kept one ear tuned to what was going on in the trophy room. I was listening for voices and noises. I did hear both. It sounded to me like several people were walking about and speaking to each other. I realised it must be true that people were chasing him down to kill him. Hear me out, akka! All I wanted at the time was to save him somehow. And I wanted to know who was pursuing him. Could Idumbankaari be part of the plot? I had to find out. The idea that so many people knew about the secret passage was frightening in itself. Also, the fact that you would be staying here was great cause for worry. I wanted to send word to my father and have someone bring him here, but I could not work up the courage. If my father were to learn that *he* had come to the antapuram, why, his very life would be in danger! So, I asked him to remain where he was. I opened the door to the trophy room suddenly and entered. I saw five–six men there. They were pressing themselves against the walls. They seemed startled to see me. And seeing them all there like that, I could not help feeling frightened myself. I forced myself to push away the fear and opened my mouth to demand, as angrily as I could, who they were and what they were doing there.

'Just then, my friend Chandramati entered this room through another door and began to shout, "Amma! Amma!" It struck me that she might see him and start screaming. I decided I would see to those men later, and turned back to come into this room. But there was no one here. He had disappeared into thin air. By this time, Chandramati had entered. I asked Chandramati if anyone had been here. She said she hadn't seen anyone. I searched the room and then went back to the trophy room. But the men I had seen there were gone now. Idumbankaari alone remained, dusting the room. "Who were the people who were standing here sometime ago? Where have they gone now?" He looked surprised and said, "No one came here, amma!" I wasn't able to believe him. But Chandramati began to tease me. "Akka! You're hallucinating today! You see people where there is nobody!" Then, she told me your entourage was nearing the palace, and that my father had sent her to fetch me right away to receive you.

'So, I headed straight for the palace gates. I decided to take a shortcut through the terraces, and that's when I saw something bizarre. That Vaanar scion was crossing the courtyard and walking alongside the wall. I then saw him climb the wall using a bamboo plant as his aid. I thought I saw him jump over. I don't know if this really happened or whether I was hallucinating.'

Nandini was lost in thought. In her mind's eye, she saw the two faces she had noticed the previous evening, among the thick foliage some distance away. She had learnt that horsemen had been sent in pursuit of the men. Had they been caught yet? And if they had, would they be brought here?

'Akka! What do you make of it?' Manimeghalai asked, bringing her back to reality.

'What do *I* make of it? I think your obsession with him has driven you crazy and messed with your mind.'

'Are you mocking me like Chandramati too?'

'I'm not mocking you. You have held an entire conversation with this man and yet are not able to tell whether it was a dream or a hallucination or something that actually happened! How could *I* possibly know? Is there another secret way out of this room?'

'Not that I know of, akka!'

'He could have taken the same route as you and Chandramati and crossed the terraces, couldn't he?'

'But there were palace maids everywhere on those terraces, akka! He could not have evaded their notice.'

'It seems quite incredible. You didn't tell your father about any of this?'

'No, akka. I am not able to bring myself to tell him, both from shyness and from fear. If it turned out to be true that he was here ...'

'Yes, it's best not to tell men about such things. They won't understand either.'

'I'm not sure whether to tell my brother or not.'

'If you tell him, it will certainly end badly. Your brother is determined to marry you off to Aditya Karikalan.'

'Akka! You must help me! Kandamaaran places great faith and trust in you. He will listen to anything you say.'

'Adi penne! You're asking me to help you with something that is entirely contradictory to my own mission in coming here! How clever you are! Let's say we stop the marriage between you and Aditya Karikalar. You don't know anything about the other man, do you? How can you be sure he wants to marry you?'

'I'm not worried about that, akka! Whether he wants to marry me or not ...'

'It appears women are destined to be like this. However a man behaves, a woman in love with him is willing to lay down her life for him. Well, let's see how your fortune pans out. If another such incident, like the one yesterday, occurs, you'll tell me, won't you?'

'Whom else would I tell if not you, akka? I had a dream last night. I'd like to tell you about that too ...'

'So, your daydreams weren't enough, eh? What dream did you have at night? Did he make another appearance and trick you again?'

'No, no! This was something else. The very thought frightens me. They say dreams one has during the wee hours of the morning will come true. Is that really the case, akka?'

'Tell me about your dream and then we'll see. What do you mean by "something else"? Was it a dream about someone else?'

'It was about him! I dreamt that someone was coming to stab him. He was unarmed. But there was a dagger on the floor, its blade shining. I leapt forward so I could take it. I decided I would stab the man who was coming to attack him before he could make his move. When I went near him, I saw his face. It was my brother, Kandamaaran! I woke up screaming. I was bathed in sweat. It was a long time before my limbs stopped shaking. The dream was so vivid! Do you think this might come true, akka?'

'Adi penne! Your mind is truly a confused mess. Things that transpired in reality seem an illusion to you. And dreams seem real. What a friend I've made! I thought *I* was insane, but you're a step ahead of me!' Nandini said.

At this point, Chandramati entered the room.

'They are almost here,' she said. 'I believe they have crossed the Veeranarayana lake.'

15

ROYAL RECEPTION

The front entrance of Kadambur Sambuvarayar's palace hosted an incredible sight that evening. People had arrived en masse to see the guests arrive and they spread out like waves for as far as the eye could see. There were youth and children, householders and the elderly.

Old men and women who couldn't trust their legs to stay standing leaned on staffs for support. They were being pushed about, but they didn't care. They stood swaying, all for a glimpse of the war hero, the intrepid conqueror Aditya Karikalan.

Children pushed and shoved, trying to get to the front ranks of the audience. Young women abandoned the shyness and embarrassment that was natural to their age and elbowed strangers, not caring about making physical contact with men they didn't know, trying to get closer to the gate. As for the young men, they had no eyes or time for the women they would otherwise be trying to woo. All their attention was focused on finding vantage points from which they could gawk at the prince. Many of them were climbing the trees that surrounded the palace, while some made so bold as to try scaling the fortress walls themselves, only to be dragged down by the palace guards.

New mothers with infants on their hips braved the inconvenience caused to them by the bustling crowd. When their babies began to wail, they cooed, 'Kanne! Don't cry. The greatest warrior of this land that births courage, Tamizhagam, is going to come here. Veerapandian Thalai Konda Aditya Karikala Chozhar will stand before us! If you look upon his face, you will grow up to be a fierce fighter, a courageous leader just like him!'

The young men who already had lovers were just as eagerly narrating the exploits of the prince to those women, who listened in fascination.

At the time, the entire land was echoing with the story of Aditya Karikalan. He had been all of twelve when he had entered the battlefield for the first time. He had quelled many an enemy with his dagger. During the Battle of Sevoor, he had decimated the Pandiya army and sent its head Veerapandiyan running for cover in the desert. When he was just nineteen, he had defeated the Abaththudavigal army of the Pandiya king, found him in his hideout and lopped off his head. How could anyone not want to see him up close?

However, over the last few years, since the young prince had been crowned Yuvraj, there had been various rumours surrounding him. Some claimed that there had been a difference of opinion between father and son, and that Sundara Chozhar did not wish his eldest son to claim his title after him. Some said Aditya Karikalar intended to establish a separate kingdom with its capital in Kanchi, as the Pallavas had once done. Still others said Aditya Karikalar was angry that his father remained partial to his second son and the crown prince's brother, Arulmozhi Varman. And then there were those who rejected that notion and swore no brothers could be as close as Aditya Karikalar and Ponniyin Selvar.

The fact that the prince was not yet married was more fodder for gossip. Some said the difference of opinion between the emperor and the prince was due to Aditya Karikalar having rejected all the royal alliances that poured in for him and insisted he would marry the daughter of a temple priest and make her the queen of the empire. Others said that he had been possessed by an evil spirit because of the machinations of mantravadis from Pandiya Naadu, which was why several of the suzerain kings did not want him to remain heir to the throne.

Irrespective of what was said and what wasn't, everyone was eager to see the prince in the flesh. And so, when news had spread that Aditya Karikalar would arrive at the Kadambur palace that evening, everyone from every village in the vicinity made a beeline for the palace. It was a grand ocean of people, spread like a giant carpet before the palace, a carpet made up of thousands upon thousands of human heads and bodies. And as their voices rose into the air, one might have mistaken the sound for the roar of the ocean waves.

And every time the palace guards opened the gate for someone who had right of entry and then slammed it shut on the front ranks of the spectators, who tried to push past, the guards would shove them away, only to be hit with more waves of people, charging and receding, ebbing and flowing, just like the waves.

Finally, someone perched high up on a tree shouted, 'There! He's coming! They're here!'

'Where? Where?' a thousand voices cried back.

A lone horse was speeding towards the palace. The animal made straight for the crowd, showing no signs of halting. The townsfolk hurriedly moved backwards to make a path for the horseman, afraid they would be crushed underfoot.

'Ilam Sambuvarayan!' they shouted in greeting.

Yes, it was indeed the heir to Sambuvarayar, Kandamaaran. He ignored the questions the crowd screamed to him and rode his horse right up to the palace, where Sambuvarayar and Periya Pazhuvettaraiyar were waiting to receive the prince.

Kandamaaran jumped off his horse and bowed before them in greeting. Then, he said, 'The prince is coming. But his mind seems off. He flies into a rage all of a sudden. I came ahead expressly to warn you. We must give him a proper reception. If he says something provocative, you must be patient and respond politely.'

Having told them this, he looked searchingly towards the terraces. The women of the palace were waiting on the balconies and verandahs. Kandamaaran entered the palace courtyard, went inside the building and climbed a set of stairs. Once he had reached the terrace where the women were standing, he ignored everyone else and made straight for Nandini Devi.

He said, 'Devi, I have fulfilled your wishes. I have escorted the prince here. There he is! But he's behaving like an elephant in musth. I have no idea how we're going to handle him!'

'Aiya! Why do you worry on that account? The elephant in musth will be brought under control soon enough with the bull-hooks that are your sister's eyes!'

'Akka! What sort of talk is this?' Manimeghalai said.

Kandamaaran intervened with, 'Manimeghalai! There is nothing wrong in what the Pazhuvoor Rani said. You must have done some great good in a past birth to be blessed with such an intrepid warrior as Aditya Karikalar for your husband!'

Before Manimeghalai could respond, Nandini asked, 'Aiya, is the prince accompanied by anyone else?'

'Yes, indeed. Parthibendra Pallavan and Vandiyadevan are with him.'

Nandini looked pointedly at Manimeghalai and said, 'Who is this Vandiyadevan? The man you said was your dear friend?'

'Indeed, the dear friend who stabbed me in the back and tried to kill me. He appeared out of nowhere and joined our entourage on the banks of the Vellaaru. I kept quiet out of consideration for the prince. If Karikalar had not been there, Vandiyadevan would have fallen prey to my sword!'

'Anna! If it were true that he tried to kill you, why would he come to this palace?' Manimeghalai asked.

'Kanne! You don't get involved. These are the matters of men. They will fall out and make up, be the worst of enemies and then the best of friends,' Nandini said.

Kandamaaran smiled and said, 'Nothing of the sort. I had to hold myself back because of the prince. Oho! Look at them bringing basket upon basket of flowers. The rain of petals you shower upon the prince will wash away his temper and calm him down. There he is! I'll head downstairs!'

With that, he ran back down the stairs.

From the terrace where the women were gathered, they could see something like a whirlpool in the sea of people, twirling its way towards the gate. And like a little boat caught in that whirlpool, three horsemen appeared and disappeared from vision. The whirlpool made its way to the palace gates and eventually entered.

Aditya Karikalar, Vandiyadevan and Parthibendran were the horsemen. The rest of the entourage, the soldiers and aides on horseback and on elephants, had all been stalled by the crowd. When the three horses appeared at the gate, the crowd roared in welcome.

At the same time, twenty perigai drums, two hundred kombus, three hundred thaarais and five hundred thambattais sounded out their greeting even as the crowd tried to drown out the instruments. However, the instruments held their own, eventually silencing the crowd. They played for a while and then stopped abruptly. In the sudden hush, the crier mounted one of the terraces and shouted:

'Manumandaka of the Surya Vamsam; and Sibi Chakravarti who sacrificed his own flesh to save the life of a dove; his descendant Raja Kesari; his son Parakesari; Manuneethi Chozhan who sacrificed his son's life to serve justice to a bereaved cow; Karikaal Peruvalaththaan who flew the tiger flag from the Himalayas; Nalankilli; Nedunkilli; Perunarkilli; their descendant Killi Valavan; Koperunjozhar who built seventy-two Shiva temples; their descendant who bore ninety and six battle scars, Pazhaiyarai Vijayalaya Chozhar; his son Aditya Chozhar, who built eighty-two Shiva temples along the banks of the Kaveri, from Sasyamalai to Puharnagar; his son Parantaka Chozha Chakravarti who conquered Madurai and Eezham and built a golden mandapam at the Thillai Chidambaram temple; his son Arinjaya Devar who decimated the armies of Irattai Mandalam's Kannar Devan and conquered Aatroor; his son Pazhaiyarai Parantaka Sundara Chozha Chakravarti, who rules from Eezham to Seetpuli Naadu; his elder son, the heir to the emperor, the Mahatanda Nayagar of the Northern Front, the Yuvaraja Chakravarti, Beheader of Veerapandiyan, Aditya Karikala Chozhar has made his entrance! Paraak! Paraak!'

His voice was as thunder.

The moment he stopped, another crier standing next to him said:

'The king of Kollimalai; the great hero Valvil Ori who felled a lion and bear and deer and boar with a single arrow; the descendant of this dynasty, Rajathi Raja Rajamarthanda Veera Gambhira Sambuvarayan; the guardian of the Veeranarayana Eri and sworn friend of the Chozha clan; commander of a five-thousand-strong army; he humbly asks the royal prince and elder son of the emperor, Aditya Karikalar, to grace his small palace by staying as a guest here. May the scion of the Chozha clan have a wonderful stay here!'

At this, the shower of flowers began from the terraces. Aditya Karikalan and Vandiyadevan glanced up. Among all the beautiful women gathered there, Vandiyadevan could only see one face—that of the smiling Manimeghalai. He smiled too. Then, as if realising he had committed a grave error, he turned to look in a different direction.

In the meantime, Aditya Karikalan—who had also glanced upwards—became even more agitated than before. He jumped off his horse. His companions followed suit. The instruments started booming out a second welcome. The crowd roared too.

The guests and those who had been waiting to receive them entered the inner courtyard. The palace gates were slammed shut at once with a 'padaar-padaar'.

Aditya Karikalan turned back and said, 'Why are they slamming the doors shut right away? Are they going to imprison me here, in the same manner they have imprisoned my father in the Thanjavur palace? What about my entourage?'

Sambuvarayar and Periya Pazhuvettaraiyar were too stunned to respond.

The latter recovered first and said, 'Komagane! The millions of hearts that beat for you and your father in Chozha Naadu have already imprisoned you within themselves. Why would anyone else seek to imprison you?'

'Ilavarase! How will this little hut bear the onslaught of all the people who seek a darshan of you? Even now, the trees on either side of the road are being crushed under the weight of the people climbing the branches for a glimpse of you, the groves look like Madhuvanam after the Vanara army finished with it. Once the people have dispersed, your entourage will be escorted inside. Until then, there are servants here waiting to do your bidding, to bring you whatever you need and do anything else the members of your entourage might.'

At this, there was another roar from the spectators.

Karikalan turned to Kandamaaran and said, 'Where are the steps that lead to the terrace?'

Kandamaaran pointed them out, and Karikalan made straight for the stairs, leaving his three friends to run to catch up with him.

Sambuvarayar turned to Pazhuvettaraiyar and said, 'What have we done? We've practically paid to buy a shani[1] that was on its way past us! He doesn't seem to be in his right mind at all! We shouldn't have listened to the youngsters and got into this!'

'What is going to happen that is so terrible? If things work out as we wish, it will be good for us. If not, the situation remains as is,' Pazhuvettaraiyar said.

'I'm not talking about what we hope will happen. Things mustn't go awry when he's staying here, under my roof. None of the omens is right. And he's arrived like an elephant in musth. He's got rage on his face and venom on his tongue!'

'There are days when one must grit one's teeth and remain patient. Parthibendra Pallavan will help keep him in check. The other young man with him ... I don't like him one bit. I have my suspicions about him. He might well be a spy. Do you remember, he had come here when we last met at the palace, all of us together? And he was the man we saw standing under the tree some distance from the palace last evening!'

'He's a friend of my son's, so we don't have to worry about him. But why are they rushing to the terrace where the women are? Should we go with them too?'

These words were overheard by Parthibendra Pallavan, who had turned back from the steps and by now returned to the spot where the two suzerain kings were speaking.

'Aiya! Whatever other suspicions you may nurse about the prince, you need have no worry on account of his behaviour with women. He does not so much as glance at them,' he said.

Pazhuvettaraiyar smiled and said, 'But if that is the case, how will the goal we hope to achieve by inviting him here be met?'

'That depends on the fortune of Sambuvarayar's daughter and that of the Chozha empire.'

'Parthibendra! Leave aside Manimeghalai's fortune for a moment. Why is the prince so angry? Why does he talk with so much spite? It strikes me that I'll be happy as long as you take him away from here in a calm state!' Sambuvarayar said.

'The prince was quite cheerful until we reached the banks of the Vellaaru. There, Vandiyadevan and some Vaishnavite joined us. They must have said something to him. The prince's mood has changed since then.'

'We thought as much. What do we do next? That young troublemaker is part of the entourage now.'

'Please be patient. I'll sort everything out. I have a bone to pick with that troublemaker too. I'll get to it when the time is right,' Parthibendran said.

When Aditya Karikalan and the other two men reached the terrace, the women were about to come down the stairs.

Karikalan turned to Kandamaaran and said, 'My friend, is it proper to make the women come to the terrace and wait for us? It is we who should seek them out in their quarters and greet them, isn't it?'

He bowed to the women and then stepped aside to give them way.

As each passed them, he asked Kandamaaran who the lady was.

When it was Nandini's turn, he said, 'Oh! It's the Pazhuvoor Ilaiya Paatti![2] Has she really graced us with her presence? How happy I am!'

Nandini said nothing, but fixed her sharp eyes on Karikalan before leaving. The force of her glare made Karikalan's body quake slightly. But he recovered right away and turned to the next in line, who was Manimeghalai. 'Oho! This must be your sister Manimeghalai. She looks like the Gandharva maidens in paintings! You must find a suitable groom and get her married soon!'

Manimeghalai turned her face to the floor from embarrassment, but couldn't contain a shy smile, nor hold back a sideways glance at Vandiyadevan before she ran downstairs.

Once all the women had gone, Karikalan went to the front of the terrace.

The crowd below, which had just begun to disperse, went berserk upon seeing him and began to roar and swell again, coming towards the palace in waves.

Aditya Karikalan spotted the crier sitting by himself on one of the benches on the terrace and signalled for him to come close. Once the crier had rushed to him, Aditya Karikalan told him to make a series of announcements to the people.

The crier sounded the perigai drum a few times. He then signalled for the spectators to be quiet. Having listed Aditya Karikalar's epithets and titles and ancestors once more, he shouted, 'This great Chozha prince will grace the Kadambur palace for up to a week, or even ten days. He will visit all the towns nearby. He will speak directly to the people of those towns and hear their problems!'

At this, the crowd let out such a roar that all the noise that had preceded this faded into silence by comparison. There were cheers and hurrahs and applause, all so loud that the sound of gushing water from all seventy-four sluice gates of the Veeranarayana Eri was indiscernible in the uproar.

Sambuvarayar, Pazhuvettaraiyar and Parthibendran had remained at their spot.

Aditya Karikalan went up to them and said, 'Parthibendra! Why did you stay here? Have you joined these old men in their conspiracy?'

The two old men looked at the prince, startled. Amusement was writ across his face.

Sambuvarayar gathered himself and said, 'Komagane! You spoke of prison sometime ago. And now you speak of conspiracy. I promise that for as long as you are a guest in this hut of mine, not the tiniest hint of danger will dare approach you! It will have to cross my lifeless body before it nears you.'

'Aiya! Do you think I'm afraid that I am in danger? I did not hold such a fear even when I was surrounded by a hundred thousand Pandiya soldiers. Why would I worry when I am surrounded by dear friends? But please don't refer to this palace of yours as a hut! Aha! How high the walls that surround the palace are! And how strong! They're even larger than the walls around the Thanjavur palace! Against which enemies have you fortified the palace so formidably?'

'Ilavarase! We have no enemies of our own. The enemies of the Chozha clan are our enemies. And the friends of the Chozha clan are our friends!'

'Your oath brings me much joy. Please do tell your son Kandamaaran this. He considers my friend Vandiyadevan an enemy. Isn't that a grave error?' Aditya Karikalan said.

Hearing this, Kandamaaran hung his head.

16

OF MALAYAMAN'S ANXIETIES

Aditya Karikalan walked through the extensive verandah that stretched between the palace and the outer walls, looking about himself. Kandamaaran was by his side, showing him the way, and the others walked some distance behind them.

Karikalan paused at the place where a stage had been set up for the kuravai koothu.

'Oho! What is this? What is going to take place here?' he asked.

'Komagane! We'd planned to stage the kuravai koothu here, if that were to interest you …'

'Aha! Wonderful! Do stage the kuravai koothu. And villupaattu.[1] And dramas that tell the story of Karikaal Valavar and Vijayalaya Chozhar. We'll spend all day hunting in the forest, and all night in dance and song. Sambuvarayare! Do you know what my grandfather Malayaman told me? He said for as long as I am at your palace, I should not sleep at night. And you know what I said in response? "Patta![2] I don't sleep during the day. And I don't sleep at night either. It has been three years since I slept. And so, you needn't be afraid that an enemy might harm me in my sleep. They can only ever harm me when I'm awake. And which man would dare do that?" I reassured him with those words,' Karikalan said and burst out laughing.

Sambuvarayar's voice shook with anger as he said, 'Aiya! Whether you're asleep or awake, no one will … for as long as you're in this palace, no one will dare harm you!'

'Yes, yes! Who could possibly live in Kadambur Sambuvarayar's palace who intends to do me harm? Or, which outsider who intends to harm me could scale such high walls? Not even Yama! Why, Yama would be scared of Kadambur Sambuvarayar! I was simply telling you of the silly anxieties of the old man from Tirukkovalur. Some people lose their courage and fortitude as they age. But, on the other hand, look at my Pazhuvoor Pattan! What a majestic stride he has! Who could guess that he is over sixty?' Karikalan said and snickered.

Pazhuvettaraiyar decided he should respond to this, and cleared his throat.

'Look! When Periya Pazhuvettaraiyar clears his throat, it sounds like a lion's roar! The very ground shakes! Kandamaara! Vandiyadeva! Parthibendra! Think about it … do you think you'll be as fit as Pazhuvoor Pattan at his age? Perhaps you'll succeed in clearing your throats like him. But you'd never be able to bring a new woman into the antapuram at his age. Thatha! It appears you've brought Ilaiya Rani with you! I saw her when I entered. How did she make the journey? In the palanquin? Chariot? Or some other vehicle?'

Pazhuvettaraiyar interrupted and said, not without pride, 'I brought her by elephant, seated on the howdah, where everyone could see her!'

'That's exactly as it should be, thatha! Make sure you do this from now on. Don't bring her in the palanquin, in any case. Because that gives rise to all manner of rumours. There was a hilarious one! People say that my uncle Madurantakan was secretly travelling the empire in Pazhuvoor Ilaiya Rani's palanquin! This rumour has spread throughout the land!' Karikalan said and roared with laughter.

None of the others joined him. Each was troubled by his own thoughts.

Vandiyadevan was thinking, *Aiyo! What a mistake I've made! I should never have told this man everything! In his rage, he'll reveal everything to these people!*

Periya Pazhuvettaraiyar's heart was as an erupting volcano. He cleared his throat again.

But before he could speak, Parthibendran took a step forward and said, 'Komagane! I only had the privilege of meeting Pazhuvoor Ilaiya Rani for a very short time. But that was enough to show me what a devoted, dutiful, divine wife she is! If anyone were to say anything against her, he will fall prey to my sword the next moment! I swear it!'

Kandamaaran too took a step forward and said, 'I don't even need a sword! If someone were to say anything against the Pazhuvoor Ilaiya Rani, I would strangle him with my bare hands. I swear it!'

At this, Vandiyadevan took a step forward as well and said, 'I am of that persuasion too! One word against the Pazhuvoor Ilaiya Rani, and I will burn the utterer to cinders with just the glare from my eyes!'

'Ahaha! Have some patience, my friends. You seem ready to pick a fight even with me! Do you see, thatha? How these men ache to protect the dignity of Tamil women! But no one has said anything against the Pazhuvoor Ilaiya Rani. I wouldn't stand by and listen if someone were to speak ill of her, would I? I wouldn't allow him to stay alive until these three heroes reached the spot. They only speak ill of her palanquin, you see. They say that coward Madurantakan has been travelling clandestinely in her palanquin. Once a man journeys in a palanquin with the curtains drawn, it isn't a good idea for the Pazhuvoor Rani to do the same thing, is it?'

'Komagane! Why should Madurantaka Devar, the grandson of Parantaka Chakravarti and the son of Kandaradityar, travel in a closed palanquin? I don't understand ...' Parthibendra Pallavan said.

'Oh, the reason they've attributed for this is hilarious too. I believe he's travelling through the land in the closed palanquin to make allies and strike deals for his side.'

'Whatever for?'

'Whatever for, you ask? To ascend the Chozha throne after my father, apparently! Can you believe it? They say he'd even come to the Kadambur Palace some months ago, hiding in that palanquin. There was a midnight meeting of conspirators here, I hear. Parthibendra! You were with me when Tirukkovalur Kizhavanaar[3] said all this, weren't you? He even said that in his hurry to inherit the throne Madurantakan might see fit to expedite my father's journey to Heaven! Don't you remember?'

'I do remember, ilavarase! I didn't believe it then, and I don't believe one bit of it now. After going to Thanjavur and meeting your father directly ...'

'You're not alone! I don't believe it either. If I did, would I have accepted the invitation to come to the Kadambur Palace as a guest?' Karikalan said, and then burst into laughter as if something funny had just occurred to him.

Kadambur Sambuvarayar cleared his throat and said, 'Komagane! You must be aware that there is a history of enmity between Tirukkovalur Malayaman's clan and ours.'

'How could I not be? Even the Sangam poets have sung of this enmity. Malayaman Tirumudikkaari killed Valvil Ori of Kollimalai in battle. Since you are descendants of Valvil Ori, you continue to nurse that enmity.'

'Komagane! Valvil Ori's death was immediately avenged. Adiyamaan Nedumananji, who was from Valvil Ori's family, marched upon Tirukkovalr and destroyed both the town and Malayaman's Mulloor hill fort …'

'Sambuvarayare! Adiyamaan did not do that all alone. It was with my ancestor Killi Valavan's help that he defeated Malayaman. But why bring up these old stories now?'

'Even if we've forgotten these things, Malayaman has not. And he never will. He's always accusing us of something or the other and …'

'I told you, didn't I? He has got old. And senile. I'm only hoping he won't bring a large army here to ensure I don't come to harm!'

'Ilavarase! If you have the slightest suspicion on that account …' Sambuvarayar began.

'Suspicion? I? Not at all! Our Chozha clan's alliance with Malayaman is only two generations old. Whereas with the Pazhuvettaraiyar clan, it goes back six generations! The king of Pazhuvoor is here himself. Have I gone insane, to even imagine that he would conspire against the Chozha dynasty?' Karikalan said, and then broke into peals of laughter, sounding quite like a madman.

Pazhuvettaraiyar said in an authoritative voice, 'Ilavarase! I swear I would not conspire against the

Chozha dynasty. And I swear twice over that I would never conspire against dharma and justice!'

'True, true. The notion of dharma and justice does exist. I came here to pick your brain about that, actually. In our spare time, between the day's hunt and the night's revelry, let's talk about dharma and justice! Sambuvarayare! Which part of this sprawling palace have you allocated for me and my friends?' Karikalan asked.

'Aiya, we have reserved the entire guesthouse for you and the king of Pazhuvoor. I'll accommodate all the other suzerain kings in my palace itself ...'

'Oho! Suzerain kings are coming too?'

'Yes, ilavarase! All the suzerain kings in the nearby territories are keen to meet you. Many of them are coming.'

'Let them come, let them come! Let them all come! Excellent! We can all come to a decision together then. Leave aside Madurantakan's conspiracy for a moment. I intend to enter into a conspiracy with all of you. There couldn't be a more appropriate place for that than this palace!' Aditya Karikalan said.

17

POONGUZHALI'S DESIRE

Poonguzhali sailed her boat along the canal that ran from Nagapattinam to Kodikkarai. Senthan Amudan was with her. As the boat neared Kodikkarai, golden-hued thazhampoo shrubs by the banks spread their fragrance everywhere, as the flowers opened their petals. A little green parrot flew to one of the thazhampoo shrubs and sat on a flower. The impact made the flower pendulate up and down like a swing. The parrot swung along with the flower and then pecked its golden petals with its own coral-hued beak. When the boat came too close for comfort, the parrot flew off with a 'ki-ki, ki-ki'.

'If one must be born, it should be as a parrot,' Poonguzhali said.

'So you say. But who knows what worries and problems the parrot has?' Senthan Amudan said.

'Whatever worries and problems one might have, one would be able to soar high into the limitless sky. Could there be greater joy than that?' Poonguzhali said.

'Well, there are those who catch those parrots that are flying free and imprison them in cages!' Amudan said.

'True, true. Princesses living in palaces catch those free birds and imprison them in cages! Cruel rakshashis! They throw the parrots into cages and then coo to them. If I were a maid in some palace, I would poison all the parrots that are stuffed into cages. And I would poison the princesses who had them caught too.'

'Anyone who hears you say such things will call you a cruel rakshashi too.'

'Let them say what they will! I would rather be a rakshashi than a princess!'

'Why are you so furious at princesses, Poonguzhali? If you think about it, one must feel sorry for them, no? They are like caged birds too. They're imprisoned in palaces. And if they want to go outside, they cannot leave without a large escort! And they must go in secrecy too. How careful they must be! They can't get into a boat and sail off into rivers and oceans all alone like you do, can they? They can't dance about like deer without a care in the world, can they?'

'Who asks them to stay within the palace walls? Not I! If they want to, why don't they go roam the forests?'

'Wanting something isn't enough. It has to do with upbringing too, where one was born and how one was raised. You wish to fly in the sky like a parrot, but can you? You were born by the sea and raised as you were, and that's why you're able to do what you want and go where you wish. If you had been born in a palace, you could not possibly have been so free. And then, do you know what, Poonguzhali? It would surprise you. But parrots who have got used to staying in cages and being fed by princesses will not fly away even if the cage is opened. They'll fly a short distance and then return with a "kreech-kreech" and fly right back into the cage. I've seen this for myself in the palaces of Thanjai and Pazhaiyarai.'

'I would never consent to being imprisoned in a cage. If I were a parrot, I would bite off the finger of the princess who came to feed me after having me caged!'

'So, you wouldn't want to be a parrot imprisoned in a cage. You wouldn't want to be a princess imprisoned in a palace either, would you?'

'Never! I would rather drink poison and die!'

'Yes, that's best. In that case, you wouldn't want to marry a prince who lives in a palace?'

Dark clouds were filling the skies overhead. Streaks of lightning flashed in the sky every now and again. There were gentle rolls of distant thunder.

And when Poonguzhali heard what Senthan Amudan said, bolts of lightning flashed in her eyes too.

'Who told you I wished to marry a prince?' she demanded angrily.

'No one told me. The thought struck me. If you have no such desire, it's all well. Forget I said anything,' Senthan Amudan said.

Silence reigned in the boat for a while. Only the sound of the oars Senthan Amudan was plying and the croaks of frogs and the chirps of seabirds and the waves in the ocean were heard, along with occasional rumblings of thunder from the east.

Senthan Amudan cleared his throat, fortified his heart and said, 'Poonguzhali! You said Vandiyadevan had told you about my feelings for you, didn't you? Would you tell me what your feelings about this are? There, the Kodikkarai lighthouse has appeared. I won't have a chance to speak to you in private after we reach the shore. I'll have to leave for home tomorrow. I've left my mother alone for too long,' he said.

'Why should Vandiyadevan carry messages for you? Don't you have a mouth of your own? Why don't you ask me whatever you want, to my face?' Poonguzhali said.

'All right, I'll ask. Will you marry me?' Senthan Amudan asked.

'Why do you want me to marry you?'

'Because I've been secretly in love with you.'

'Does being secretly in love mean one must absolutely get married?'

'No, it doesn't mean one must absolutely do so, but that's how the world works.'

'What will you give me if I marry you? Can you give me a royal life and all the clothes and ornaments I desire and horses and elephants and palanquins and handmaidens?'

'No, but I can give you something beyond all that—a peaceful life. Listen, Poonguzhali. My hut is set in a lovely flower garden on the outskirts of Nagapattinam. Only my mother and I live there. If you were to come there, your life would change. My mother will shower her love and affection on you. When dawn breaks, the two of us can go pluck flowers in the garden and string together the most beautiful garlands. I will take the garlands to the Thanjai Thalikulaththaar and Durga Parameshwari temples. In the meantime, you can bathe in the lotus pond in our garden and help my mother with the housework. In the evenings, the three of us can fetch water from the pond for the plants in the garden. I will then teach you divine Tamil padigams which are sweeter than honey. If you sing them in your lovely voice, your tongue will sweeten from uttering the words and my ears from hearing them. If we so wish, we can go from temple to temple, singing those songs before the deities. That will bring joy to the worshippers at the temples. Poonguzhali! What could be a more pleasant, more joyful life than this? Think about it!'

Having heard him out, Poonguzhali broke into peals of laughter.

'Amuda! You told me about a life that you consider pleasant and joyful. But do you know what kind of life I desire? I wish to fly to the skies and marry Indra, the lord of the devas! I wish to ride with him on the Airavata across the clouds in the sky. I wish to see him shoot those clouds with the vajrayudha and watch hundreds of bolts of lightning emerge from those clouds and tear the skies. And you know how thunderbolts fall on trees or into the ocean? I wouldn't waste them like that. I would aim them at the palaces where kings and queens and princes and princesses live. I will rejoice at the sight of those palaces turning to dust.

'And if Indra isn't too keen on marriage, I'll turn to Vayu. I'll tell him it doesn't matter that he already has plenty of wives, I would like to add to that number. And that's it … from the moment I marry him, this world will see tornadoes and thunderstorms and hurricanes all year round. Enormous trees will be uprooted and will fall on these palaces and mansions, crushing them and their inhabitants. Ships at sea will shatter into pieces in tempests, and the people on those ships will flail in the waves, suffering every moment of their deaths. If there are princes and princesses among them, I will let them sink to the bottom of the sea and probably spare everyone else. And if the god of wind hesitates to marry me, I will turn to the god of fire. Once I'm Agni's wife ... need I say more? The entire world will burn in the blaze ...!'

'Poonguzhali, that's enough! Stop it! Some bitterness inside you is making you spit out such things. You are not conscious of what you're saying. I erred in speaking of marriage to you without understanding your state of mind. Please forgive me for it. It is only God who can remove the bitterness from your heart and heal you. I will pray day and night for His grace!' Senthan Amudan said.

Poonguzhali suddenly rose from her seat. She peered at a tree on the banks of the river. Senthan Amudan turned to look too.

A woman's face appeared among the branches of the tree. Senthan Amudan was shocked by her resemblance to his mother. He then realised it must be his Periamma, who Poonguzhali had said lived in Bhoota Theevu.

Poonguzhali leapt off the boat and on to the shore, and began to run towards the woman.

18

THE FLYING ARROW

Poonguzhali looked at the Oomai Rani, half-hidden behind a tree on the shore. Encountering her like this, at an unexpected place and hour, startled Poonguzhali for a moment. She knew that her aunt did not like meeting strangers. Senthan Amudan was on the boat. Would her Aththai run away when she saw Poonguzhali was not alone?

She had barely completed the thought before her aunt took off at a run. Poonguzhali jumped onto the shore and ran to an elevated spot. She saw her aunt disappearing into the forest some distance away.

Senthan Amudan had joined her by now.

'Poonguzhali! Poonguzhali! Who was that, standing here a moment ago?' he asked.

'Couldn't you tell, Amuda?'

'Not for sure. But, perhaps ...'

'Yes, my Aththai! And your Periyamma, whom you thought was dead all this while!'

'Yes, I thought I could spot a resemblance to Amma.'

'Oh, please, you're just saying that. Chinna Aththai and Periya Aththai look nothing like each other. There is no similarity in their natures either. That's like comparing a cow tethered in one's backyard to a lioness roaming free!'

'Right, that's as may be. But why did the lioness take off at a run upon seeing you?'

Poonguzhali laughed and said, 'She ran upon seeing *you*! She doesn't like meeting strangers.'

'But I'm not a stranger, am I?'

'How would Aththai know who you are? Until she realises, she will hesitate to come anywhere close. Once I tell her you're her nephew, she won't run away.'

'Poonguzhali, what will you do now?'

'I'm going to go find Aththai.'

'Shall I come along?'

'Why?'

'To meet Periyamma in person.'

'Why should you meet Periyamma?'

Senthan Amudan had been keen to meet his Periyamma after learning something of her past from Poonguzhali. He also hoped she might help him convince Poonguzhali to marry him.

'For several reasons. But does one need a reason to want to meet his own aunt?' he asked.

Poonguzhali thought for a while and then said, 'All right, come along. It will be much harder to catch her if you're with me, but you won't stop badgering me, so let's not waste any more time. We'll secure the boat here and go.'

They hid the boat behind a thazhampoo shrub and made for the Kodikkarai forest.

'You said Periyamma would be either in Bhoota Theevu or the Lankan mainland, didn't you?'

'Yes, she divides her time between the two.'

'Does she come here often?'

'No, very rarely. She comes to check on me if I haven't been to meet her for a long time.'

'And has she come to see you now?'

'I have a feeling she's here for some other reason.'

'What could that be?'

'Perhaps to see whether her beloved adopted son has drowned in the sea or reached the shore safely. Aththai knows there was a tempest after the prince boarded the ship, no?'

'If Arulmozhi Varmar is her adopted son, who is her actual son?'

'I don't know. But I will find out sooner or later.'

'Is her actual son even alive?'

'True, he might be dead, who knows?' Poonguzhali said.

After a while, she said, 'Amuda! You saw Aththai and said she bore some resemblance to your mother. Does someone else's face come to mind?'

'I have a vague feeling that she does remind me of someone else. But I can't tell for sure. It is as if it were hidden behind clouds.'

'Have you seen Pazhuvoor Ilaiya Rani often?'

'I've seen her now and then, yes. Oh! It didn't occur to me until you just mentioned it, but Periyamma *does* look like Nandini Devi! How strange! How is that possible, Poonguzhali? And how did you notice the resemblance?'

'I meet Aththai often. And I saw the Pazhuvoor Ilaiya Rani only some days ago, right here in Kodikkarai. Their facial resemblance struck me right away.'

'What could the reason be?'

'That's another thing I'll find out sooner or later. I'm planning to ask Aththai about it when I meet her today.'

'But Aththai is mute. How will she respond?'

'Don't you speak to your mother?'

'Yes. Through signs and gestures. But I've been doing it all my life. Even so, I struggle when I have to convey something out of the ordinary.'

'Periya Aththai and I talk through signs and gestures too. And what we can't convey through those, we tell through paintings.'

'What an awful thing for both sisters to be deaf-mute! How much sorrow it must have brought their parents!'

'And that's not all. Throughout their childhood, the two sisters fought all the time. That's why our grandfather went away with Periya Aththai and settled in Bhoota Theevu. He was particularly fond of her. Some astrologer had told him when she was an infant that she was born to be queen. When he found out she was mute, he was devastated.'

They entered the forest as they spoke, and began their search for the Oomai Rani. But the hours passed, and yet there was no sign of her.

'Amuda! We aren't able to find Aththai because of your presence. She must have hidden herself somewhere after seeing you.'

'Just my luck. Nothing I want materialises. All right, shall I leave then?'

'How will you find your way out? It is I who must guide you.'

At that very moment, a strange cry rose from inside the forest. It sounded neither human nor bestial. The cry was repeated a couple of times. A herd of deer went flying in the direction from which the voice came.

Poonguzhali thought for some time, and then said, 'Amuda! Follow me silently.'

The two of them walked as quietly as they could in the direction from which the cry had come. It was not long before they came upon a bizarre sight.

The Oomai Rani was leaning against a tree, holding out some grass. The deer stood all around her, eating from her hands. On her shoulders, she straddled a little fawn, who was staring at her face with beautiful, large eyes.

Poonguzhali and Amudan stood in silence, gazing upon this incredible sight. It was the fawn that first spotted them, and jumped off Oomai Rani's shoulders and onto the ground right away. This drew the attention of the other deer to the intruders. The animals stood poised to run if they approached. Finally, the Oomai Rani saw them too, and let out another strange sound from her throat. At this, the entire herd of deer fled.

'The only language Aththai doesn't speak is that of humans. She can communicate with every other species in their languages,' Poonguzhali said, and began to communicate with her aunt through gestures of the hand.

This time, her aunt did not run. She responded to Poonguzhali with gestures of her own.

Then, Poonguzhali went up to her. Her aunt embraced her and kissed the top of her head. Senthan Amudan remained waiting some distance away.

The two women spoke in sign language for some time, and then Poonguzhali beckoned Amudan to join them.

At first, the Oomai Rani looked him up and down a few times, and then placed her palm on his head as if to bless him. She then took her hand away and grabbed Poonguzhali, urgently leading her somewhere. Senthan followed them.

The three of them reached the shore. The Oomai Rani sat down and conveyed something to Poonguzhali, who then said, 'Amuda, come let's go home. Aththai refuses to come with us. She wants us to bring her some food instead.'

The two of them made for the lighthouse.

'Poonguzhali, what are your plans now?' Amudan asked.

'I did want to come to Thanjai with you. But now, I can't. Aththai wants to meet her beloved adopted son. So, I'll have to go back to Nagapattinam. It's best you don't come along. I have a lot of questions for Aththai, and she'll only answer them in private.'

Senthan Amudan heaved a sigh and said, 'Just my luck. All right then, I'll say goodbye right away.'

'No, no! Come home, have some food and take your leave of everyone at home. Otherwise, they'll start fighting with me.'

On their way to the lighthouse, they came across another strange sight. In the shadow of a bush, partially hidden from sight, stood a man and woman, talking.

Aha! It seems to be Anni Rakkammaal, Poonguzhali thought. *So, her secret meetings continue. Who is that with her? A spy from Pandiya Naadu? Or someone else?*

Rakkammaal parted the bush and stepped out. Her eyes fell on Poonguzhali, and she seemed startled. But she recovered quickly, and approached the two of them.

'Poonguzhali! Where were you all this while? Your father and brother have been so anxious!' she said.

'Why? Is this the first time I've left home?'

'This time, you took your Aththai's son along, no? They were worried that you've eloped and married him!'

'Anni! How many times have I told you not to talk this sort of rubbish! If you do this again ...'

'No, penne, I won't! What do I care if you marry your Aththai's son? Or a prince for that matter? Your Periya Aththai came in search of you from Lanka. Did you meet her?'

'No, not yet,' Poonguzhali said.

The moment she got a chance to speak to Amudan alone, she whispered, 'Amuda! Careful! Anni is in cahoots with those spies from Pandiya Naadu. She'll try to draw you out and get information from you about what we've been up to. Don't answer her!'

'I might as well join the mutes in our family for whatever time I'm here,' Amudan said.

~*~

That afternoon, Poonguzhali left for Nagapattinam with her aunt. Typically, she would feel calm and relaxed in the Oomai Rani's company. The two of them had a rapport, and it was as if their hearts were in sync. But this time, that sense of peace eluded her.

She often thought about how she had rowed Ponniyin Selvan along the same route, when he had been burning with fever. When it struck her that she had gone to all that trouble, only for him to choose a princess over her, she felt a stab of pain in her chest.

The manner in which she had practically pushed Senthan Amudan away, insisting he go back home, also made her feel guilty.

There was another thought that troubled her. It was what her father had said as she was leaving. Uncharacteristically, he had warned her against setting off alone. 'My child!' he had said. 'It would be a good idea not to go back and forth so much. All sorts of strangers have been frequenting this place. No one seems to know why they're here or at whose instance. People speak of conspiracy in the palace corridors. Please don't get drawn into such things. Our family is obligated to serve the Chozha clan. We are forever indebted to them for many, many things. Don't forget that!'

Her sister-in-law's secret rendezvous made Poonguzhali uneasy. Perhaps those strangers had been looking for Poonguzhali, in the hope that she would lead them to Prince Arulmozhi Varmar? How terrible it would be if she was the one who gave him away!

As if all this were not enough, she could hear rustling sounds coming from the banks. There was no breeze at all. It was as if the wind was being held ransom. What was causing the rustling in the undergrowth then? The Oomai Rani was, naturally, untroubled by all this for she couldn't hear anything. There was no point in asking her what she made of it.

Yet, her aunt had some superpowers. Her eyesight was so sharp it all but made up for her deafness. And she seemed to have a sixth sense. Surely, as long as the Oomai Rani was around, nothing could happen to either of them?

But then … her Aththai was also looking towards the shore, with a worried expression. Were they being pursued then?

Soon, though, she realised why her aunt had been looking at the shore. And it came as a relief.

A group of five or six deer stood among the bushes along the bank, peering at the boat. No, they were not peering at the boat, but at the Oomai Rani! Aha … what beautiful creatures deer were! Why had the same God who had created these lovely animals also chosen to create such an ugly species as the human? Unworthy beings! Why, there were people who actually hunted deer! How could one bring oneself to kill these innocent, beautiful animals? As she marvelled at the deer, Poonguzhali was so lost in her thoughts that she stopped rowing.

The boat came to a halt.

All of a sudden, a guttural scream emerged from the Oomai Rani's throat, different from what Poonguzhali and Amudan had heard in the morning. There was panic and urgency in that cry, as if she was trying to warn someone. The deer sensed her panic and began to run.

At that moment, they heard the whizz of an arrow being shot. The arrow flew and hit one of the deer, which let out a moan. The Oomai Rani leapt from the boat onto the shore and made for the wounded deer.

As she was nearing the animal, there was a mad rustling in the bushes. Seven or eight men suddenly surrounded her. Many of them held spears. Not far off stood Rakkammaal, who must have guided them to the spot.

The Oomai Rani tried to escape, but couldn't move. When she realised it was pointless, she stood still. Two men stepped forward and bound her arms with rope.

All this occurred within seconds.

As soon as Poonguzhali saw them tying her aunt up, she leapt onto the shore herself, oar in hand to serve as a weapon.

Five men broke away from the group and ran towards Poonguzhali. They caught her and carried her to the boat, where they bound her tightly with rope. Then, they left along with the Oomai Rani.

19

LAUGHTER AND FIRE

Poonguzhali tried with all her strength to free herself from the ropes that bound her to the boat. It proved to be a difficult task. The sandala paavis! They had twisted the rope in on itself several times and made a series of knots. Poonguzhali's pen knife was at the bottom of the boat. If she could free just one hand, she would reach for it and cut off the rest of the ropes. But the paavis had wound the rope around her back and ensured that her hands were secured. Poonguzhali managed to lever herself so she could bend down to the bottom of the boat and take the knife between her teeth. Holding it with her pearly whites, she began to grind the knife against the rope. She managed to break it at one point, which loosened the grip the rope had on her arms. She freed one arm with great difficulty. It was not hard to cut off the rest of the ropes after that.

It took her about a naazhigai to free herself. By this time, she could hear footsteps approaching the banks. Then, a shadow appeared. It must be one of her captors! Or perhaps they had belatedly sent someone to ensure that she did not free herself.

The moment she saw him, Poonguzhali decided to kill him. With this in mind, she aimed her knife.

But what a disappointment!

'Poonguzhali! Poonguzhali!' cried Senthan Amudan's voice.

Then, her cousin's terrified face appeared at the shore.

Poonguzhali tucked her knife into her waistband.

Amudan had spotted her too.

'Poonguzhali! Are you alive?' he asked, running towards her.

'My being alive seems to pose some difficulty to you. Come and kill me yourself if you wish. But where will you find the courage to do something like that?' Poonguzhali said.

'Shiva! Shiva! What horrible words you speak? Why would I kill you? It is you who is killing me with your words!'

'Then, why didn't you show up a little earlier? Do you know how hard it was for me to free myself?' Poonguzhali said, trying to stand up. Her feet were stuck in the ropes and she stumbled. Senthan Amudan caught her before she fell.

'Aiyayo! How those blackguards have tied you up! Your entire body is red and swollen from the ropes!'

'How much concern you show now! Why didn't you turn up earlier?'

'You're asking me the same question again! How would I know you were in such danger? You chased me away, so I went off ...'

'Then why did you come back? To see whether I was dead so you could cremate my body before going on your way?'

'The poison that was stuck in Shiva Perumaan's throat seems to be oozing out of your tongue! Your Anni said you might be in danger, so I came running. What a reward for my pains!'

By this time, Poonguzhali had stepped off the boat and onto the shore. 'I was aiming this knife at you. You got away. Now, I'm going to use this same knife on my Anni before I do anything else. Where is that sandali?'

'Why change the target of your rage from me to your Anni? Why are you so angry with her? Was it wrong for her to tell me you could be in trouble?'

'She's the one who got Aththai caught! You also saw her whispering among the bushes with someone else, no?'

'You're wrong. I don't know whom your Anni was sharing which secret with, but I know for sure she played no part in getting your Aththai caught. The same people who forcibly carried away Aththai had tied your Anni to a tree. And they hit her on the head too. She was bleeding.'

'What a joke! I don't believe this at all. She has tricked you. Well, let that be. Tell me why you came back, where you saw Anni ... everything, from start to finish!' Poonguzhali demanded.

Senthan Amudan told her the whole story. He had been going towards Thanjavur. His steps had been heavy. He had not been of a mind to leave Poonguzhali behind. As he was walking slowly on the road, a scream rose from the forest nearby. There seemed to be a great commotion somewhere deep in the woods. It sounded as if several people were walking at great speed. Senthan Amudan slipped behind a tree so he could watch the newcomers unseen. A group of seven, perhaps eight, soldiers bearing spears emerged from the forest and got onto the Rajpath. He thought he saw a woman in their midst. When someone moved slightly, he discerned that the woman looked like Poonguzhali's Aththai. Senthan Amudan decided he must be hallucinating.

Once the men had disappeared, a woman's voice persistently rose from the forest, sounding as if she was crying for help.

Senthan Amudan's first instinct was to walk away. *Why get involved? Let me just go my way*, he said to himself.

But his heart wouldn't allow it. He had to see if someone was in trouble, and then see whether he could help. He made for the voice.

He found Rakkammaal tied to a tree. Blood had poured from a wound on her head, and streamed down her face. She was an awful sight. Amudan was almost too frightened to approach her. He had to fortify himself before freeing her from the ropes.

'Who did such a cruel thing to you? And why? Who were those people who got onto the Rajpath from the forest just now? And there was a woman with them! Who is she?' he asked.

'Oh, thambi, they have taken your Periyamma with them. I tried to stop them, and they beat me up and tied me to a tree. Your mama's daughter was with your Periyamma on the boat. They dragged your Periyamma from the boat. I don't know what became of Poonguzhali! Go, run, find out if she's all right!' Rakkammaal said.

Just as Senthan Amudan was breaking into a run to go to Poonguzhali's aid, Rakkammaal said, 'Thambi, hold on for a moment! Where were Poonguzhali and that Oomai Pisaasu headed? Do you know? Why did they leave you behind? And where are you going by yourself?'

Senthan Amudan did not like her tone, particularly her referring to his aunt as 'Oomai Pisaasu'. Her questions seemed suspicious.

'I'll tell you later!' he said, before running towards the canal.

All through, he was haunted by the fear that they might have beaten, or even killed, Poonguzhali. To see her alive and relatively unhurt was an enormous relief.

Having finished this narration, Senthan Amudan said, 'Poonguzhali, don't you agree now that it was wrong for you to be angry with your Anni?'

'That's what it sounds like, from what you just said … Where did you leave her? Let's go there and see.'

'How can we be sure that she will still be there?'

'Well, if not at that exact spot, she must be nearby. If not, she'll come looking for us. Amuda! Anni asked where Aththai and I were headed, didn't she?'

'Yes, she did.'

'And you didn't answer? You're sure?'

'Yes, I'm sure. I was so angry at her for saying "Oomai Pisaasu" that I walked away without answering her questions.'

'Even if she sweet-talks you from now on, don't answer anything she asks! Why does she want to know where we were headed? Amuda! We can't be certain that there is no link between Anni and Aththai's captors. They might have got their information from her, and once they had what they were after, they probably decided to get rid of her by beating her up and tying her to a tree. Even if that was not the case, she must have been following us. How could her intentions be good? Don't get fooled by her. Be careful and make sure you don't trust her blindly!'

'Poonguzhali, you often say your brother goes mute in your Anni's presence, no? I'll follow the example he has set. You do all the talking.'

That made Poonguzhali burst into laughter.

'The sound of you laughing is music to my ears, as sweet as Tirunaavukkarasar's Devara padigams ...' Amudan said.

'I laughed by accident. Don't be fooled. My heart is ablaze. A fire burns within me.'

'This blaze in your heart will be extinguished by the flood of God's compassion,' Senthan Amudan said.

20

THE PHYSICIAN'S SON AGAIN

For a while, Poonguzhali and her cousin walked in silence along the forest path.

Then, Poonguzhali sighed heavily and said, 'Amuda! I have a feeling you and I have a connection that transcends births ...'

'Who cares about our previous births? Tell me if you can think of something good about our connection in this one.'

'They say the connections we have in one life will carry on to the next. That must be true. I thought I had seen you for the last time when I bade you goodbye, and then, before two naazhigais could pass, you came right back!'

'Don't worry too much on that account. Once we have got onto the Rajpath, I'll be on my way to Thanjavur. And you can go wherever you wish.'

'I'm not going to leave you alone now. After speaking to Anni, I'm going to go with you to

Thanjavur. I'm going to find a way to get Aththai out of the trouble she is in. I'm going to go to the Chakravarti and seek redress ...'

'Poonguzhali, do you think it's that easy to meet the Chakravarti? People like us cannot even enter the Thanjavur fortress!'

'Why not? If they don't open the gates for me, I'll break them open! And if I can't do that, I'll jump over the walls!'

'And what will you do about the sentries who are standing on guard?'

'I'll start such a riot that they will escort me to the Chakravarti themselves!'

'No one can bully Chinna Pazhuvettaraiyar into bending to one's will! Not even Yama can enter the Chakravarti's chambers without his permission, they say. Some people say that's why the emperor is still alive.'

'If I can't meet the Chakravarti, I'll meet the Pazhuvettaraiyar brothers and demand redressal! And if they don't grant it, I will go to the prime minister! And if that doesn't work either, I will go to the queens of Pazhaiyarai and appeal to them! I will not stay put until I learn what has become of my Aththai. I will not sleep a wink until they make amends for this injustice that has been done to her! Anni referred to my Aththai as "Oomai Pisaasu", didn't she? Well, I will turn into a pisaasu too, and I will roam the entire land, screaming for justice. Amuda, will you come with me?'

'Indeed I will, Poonguzhali! If that is what you want, I certainly will! But why do you mess up your mind like this, imagining all sorts of things? You've jumped fifty steps ahead, when the priority is to find out where your Aththai is and rescue her! We must free her from her captors, no? We must inform your father and brother and everyone else, no?'

'Amuda! My Aththai has divine powers. No one can do her any harm. She will burn them to ashes with one glance, as Damayanti burnt the hunter.[1] So I'm not too worried about her. But for such a terrible thing to happen in broad daylight in the Chozha empire ... they say that this empire has seen Dharma Rajyam since the time of Parantaka Chakravarti. Under the rule of the great Shiva devotee Kandaraditya Devar, they say, cows and tigers would drink peacefully from the same pond. They boast that while Sundara Chozhar sits on the throne, young women can roam the land freely whether it is day or night. And in this empire, an old woman—a deaf-mute woman, so innocent and helpless—has been abducted by a gang of armed men. I'm not worried about my Aththai's safety. But what happened to her today could happen to me tomorrow. Or to any maiden in this land. Isn't it?'

Senthan Amudan said, 'True, such lawlessness does prevail in this land these days. Ever since Sundara Chozhar took to his bed, the concept of dharma has turned on its head. Maidens are unsafe, with danger waiting at every corner. So, it is best for maidens to marry as soon as possible.'

Poonguzhali burst into laughter. 'Amuda,' she said, 'if a maiden were to marry you, would you be able to protect her? Do you know how to fight with a sword?'

'I have only learnt how to make garlands from flowers and how to sing padigams to appeal to God for His grace. So what? You taught me how to ply oars and row the boat, didn't you? I'll learn how to wield the sword and wage war too. When Madurantaka Devar seeks to ascend the throne and rule this empire, why shouldn't I aspire to be a swordsman?'

By this time, they had reached the spot where Senthan Amudan had found Rakkammaal. But the lady herself was nowhere to be seen now. Amudan pointed out spots in the ground where blood had spilled from the wound on her head.

'How hard they've hit her! It's obvious that Anni was not in cahoots with those men. But we must find out for whom she was spying,' Poonguzhali said.

'My mama's daughter! Will you listen for a moment? There is no logical explanation for anything that transpired here today. It has to do with matters of great importance to the powers-that-be. And some big mystery seems to be involved. There are wheels within wheels, secrets within secrets. All of these have to do with the royal family and their rule. What do the likes of you and me have to do with all this? Why must we give it any thought and worry ourselves?'

'Amuda! Who cares how important this royal matter is or how big the mystery is? How can I not worry about something that involves my Aththai? And how can you not worry about something that involved your Periyamma?'

'Poonguzhali, I speak from the heart. I told you I saw a group of armed men with a woman in their midst, didn't I? And that she resembled Periyamma? But they didn't seem to be forcing her to come with them. Her gait suggested that she was going of her own volition.'

'That's quite possible, Amuda! It could be. My Aththai's nature is like that … she must be curious about where they're taking her. If she does not wish to go somewhere, she will find a way to escape even if she is surrounded by a thousand guards. Fortified walls and subterranean dungeons are not impermeable to her. That's why I'm not worried for her safety. My goal is simply to seek redress for the injustice that has been done to my aunt. And it is not the injustice that was visited upon her today, but the terrible injustice done to her twenty-five years ago! I will not be at peace until they make amends for it!' Poonguzhali said.

'Kadavule! What an impossible task you've set yourself!' Senthan Amudan said, with a heavy sigh.

They heard voices coming from some distance away. One appeared to belong to a woman. As Poonguzhali and Amudan left the forest for the Rajpath, they saw the speakers.

Rakkammaal's interlocutor was the Pazhaiyarai physician's son. The moment Poonguzhali saw him, her face filled with disgust.

And the moment Rakkammaal saw Poonguzhali, she cried, 'Adi penne! You've escaped? I was terrified they'd killed you! See what they've done to me? I tried to rescue your Aththai from them and they hit me so hard on the head I have this huge wound! I was asking the physician's son if he has any balm to apply on the wound.'

'If the Karaiyar's[2] daughter has been wounded, I will cure her with my herbs,' the physician's son said.

Poonguzhali didn't respond to his offer. Instead, she addressed her brother's wife and said, 'Anni! Do you know which way they went after capturing Aththai?'

'I didn't see. But the physician's son says they took the road to Thanjavur.'

'Anni! Amudan and I will follow Aththai. Tell Appa. Come, Amuda!' Poonguzhali said, and started walking away.

The physician's son interjected with, 'Poonguzhali! Hold on. You can't follow them. They had kept their horses some distance away. They are riding to Thanjavur, not walking. I have a horse. I'll go in pursuit of them. I'll ride like the wind until I find them and then tell you where they are. In return, I ask one favour of you. Tell me where you and your Aththai were headed in the boat.'

'Anni!' Poonguzhali said. 'We don't need this man's help. We're leaving. Don't forget to tell Appa.'

The physician's son would not let go. 'Aha! Look at the arrogance of the Karaiyar's daughter! She says she doesn't need my help! Penne! Why are you so angry with me? Am I the obstacle to your marrying the prince? That man for whom you tricked me, to help him evade arrest and whom you rowed out to meet the prince … that Vaanar scion is the one who pushed your beloved prince into the sea and killed him! Why take your anger out on me?' And he broke into a laugh.

Poonguzhali's eyes spat fire at the physician's son.

Then, she grabbed Senthan Amudan's hand and dragged him onto the road.

After they had walked some distance, she said, 'Amuda! Once you've learnt how to wield the sword, you must claim the life of this physician's son. He must be the first to fall prey to your sword!'

Senthan Amudan and Poonguzhali walked day and night in order to reach Thanjavur as fast as they could. They made enquiries about a group of soldiers escorting a woman along the way. Until they reached the halfway point, they were able to glean some information about which route the group had taken. After that, no one had anything to tell them. Nevertheless, they decided to go to Thanjavur and resume their search there.

The journey was an exciting one for Senthan Amudan. One reason was Poonguzhali's company. The other was that his lessons in sword-fighting had begun. He had stopped at a forge that Poonguzhali knew of, near Kodikkarai, and bought himself a dagger. He twirled it throughout the journey. Sometimes, he imagined that an opponent was standing across from him and aimed the dagger at this vision. His throws were all poor though. Eventually, Poonguzhali began to teach him how to hold the dagger and how to twirl it. This made the journey pleasant for both of them.

It was only when the Thanjavur fortress loomed before them that Poonguzhali began to worry about how she would achieve the task she had set out to do. Senthan Amudan shared her anxiety. Gaining entry into the fortress would be hard enough. How would they do the various things Poonguzhali was determined to do? Vandiyadevan's ploys and tricks came to mind. If only he had a tenth of Vandiyadevan's enterprising mind! Or, if only Vandiyadevan were here!

Senthan Amudan thought about what Vandiyadevan would do under such circumstances.

At that very moment, a closed palanquin entered the street. The sun was setting in the west, bringing a veil of darkness on the land. On the outer screen of the palanquin, they could see paintings of palm trees.

Aha! This looks like the palanquin of the Pazhuvoor Ilaiya Rani! If only we could meet her outside the walls and get a signet ring from her to gain entry! Senthan Amudan thought.

He expressed the thought to Poonguzhali, who agreed that it was a good idea. But how would they meet the Ilaiya Rani when she was inside the palanquin? Her ride was surrounded by bodyguards. They would thwart any attempt to get close to her.

'Amuda! Don't worry! The palanquin has to travel half a kaadham to reach the Thanjavur fortress. We'll find an opportunity before that!' Poonguzhali said.

And, as expected, the opportunity presented itself to them.

21

THE PRIVILEGE OF RIDING A PALANQUIN

That year, the monsoon had not set in at the usual time. Twice, clouds had loomed overhead and rain had started falling, only to stop all of a sudden. The volume of water was reducing in the Kaveri and the rivers to which it was linked. With the irrigation canals running dry, crops in the fields began to wilt.

'This is all because of the shooting star!' people said among themselves.

'It looks like evil will be visited upon this land in every possible way!'

'There is all sorts of confusion about who is in charge of the kingdom!'

'There is no news of the prince!'

'And on top of all this, it appears the skies will let us down ...'

As Senthan Amudan and Poonguzhali walked down the road, they overheard conversations of this sort among the subjects of Chozha Naadu.

The dry weather did suit the two of them.

The morning had been unbearably hot and the afternoon unbearably humid. Even walking under the trees that lined the road leading to the royal palace, they were bathed in sweat.

'It doesn't feel like Aippasi at all. It feels like the summer month of Vaigaasi,' Poonguzhali sighed.

Even so, rain was always an inconvenience on a journey, especially when one was in a hurry. So, neither complained too much.

Not long after the palanquin bearing the Pazhuvettaraiyar symbol had crossed them, a cool breeze began to blow. The leaves rustled. The skies towards the northwest started darkening. And the clouds seemed to sink lower.

Suddenly, as if an entire herd of elephants had got into musth, the clouds surged forward, jostling against each other.

The cool breeze turned into a gusty wind. Needles of rain began to shoot through the wind. And within a quarter of a naazhigai, the needles turned into waterfalls. The rain poured with such ferocity that the trees bent over. Branches broke off and crashed to the ground. The birds that had sought shelter in those trees screeched and flew off in a panic. The people who had been walking along the road too ran in every direction. Some ran to escape the wind and rain. Others ran from the fear that the falling branches would kill them. Some ran because they were terrified into flight by the thunder, which sounded like the universe was splintering into bits.

Not long after the downpour began, day gave way to dusk. Senthan Amudan and Poonguzhali gave up on the thought of entering the Thanjavur fort before nightfall. They decided it would be best to go to Senthan Amudan's house on the outskirts of the city. As darkness fell, they walked carefully, trying to talk each other out of their fears.

'Poonguzhali! You've sailed all alone on the high seas, through storms where the waves rise as high as hills. Why are you so scared of rainfall?' Senthan Amudan asked.

'Storms and rain in the middle of the sea don't send tree branches falling on our heads! The only thing that falls from the sky is thunder,' Poonguzhali said.

She had barely finished the sentence when a tree split in half right before their eyes. Another was uprooted. Senthan Amudan held Poonguzhali's hand tightly to stop her from walking further.

'It makes no sense to rush home now. There are some old mandapams on the side of the road. Let's take shelter in one of those until the rain eases off,' Senthan Amudan said.

'We can, but how will we spot the mandapams in the dark?' Poonguzhali asked.

'We'll see them when lightning strikes. We have to keep our eyes peeled for them, on either side,' Senthan Amudan said.

Just then, a blinding flash of lightning tore through the sky.

'There's a mandapam!' Senthan Amudan cried.

Poonguzhali had spotted it too. She also saw a fallen tree in the light. It appeared some people were trapped under it.

'Amuda! Did you see the fallen tree? Under it …'

'Yes, I did. Before we're victims of the same fate, let's make for the mandapam,' Senthan Amudan said, and hurried in the direction of the mandapam, dragging Poonguzhali by the hand.

They reached the mandapam and squeezed water out of their soaked clothes. Once she was done with her clothes, Poonguzhali squeezed water out of her long hair too. The water made little rivulets on the floor of the mandapam.

'Adada! We've made the mandapam wet!' Poonguzhali said.

'That's not going to affect the mandapam in any way. It won't fall sick with fever or a cold. You're soaking wet!' Senthan Amudan said.

'I was born and raised in the sea. I'm also known as "Samudra Kumari". Raindrops won't do anything to me,' Poonguzhali said.

As she said the words 'Samudra Kumari', her heart flew to the Choodamani Viharam at Nagapattinam. That was where the man who had bestowed the epithet on her was …

'Poonguzhali, my home is not far from here. As soon as the rain eases up, we'll go there. My mother will look after you there,' Senthan Amudan said, but Poonguzhali was far away, in Nagapattinam.

Again, there was a flash of lightning. The vignette they had seen earlier now appeared clearly before them. They stared in shock. An enormous banyan tree had been uprooted near the mandapam. Its various branches and roots lay in a tangled mess. Two horses and a group of five or six people were caught in the mess. Others were trying to free them. The rescuers were hurriedly removing the fallen branches.

'Aiyo!'

'Appaaa!'

'Here!'

'Help!'

'Quickly!'

'Hurry!'

The panicked voices were all but swallowed by the sound of the rain.

But something else caught the attention of Senthan Amudan and Poonguzhali. Some distance from the fallen tree was a palanquin. Only two men stood guard by it. Everyone else seemed to be engaged in the rescue operation.

'Amuda! Did you see the palanquin?' Poonguzhali asked.

'I did. It seems to be the Pazhuvoor Ilaiya Rani's!'

'If only the tree had fallen on it!'

'Kadavule! Why would you say such a thing? You said you wanted to meet the Pazhuvoor Rani and ask for her help with something, didn't you?'

'Yes, but I don't like her much.'

'And if you don't like her, a tree should fall on her, is it?'

'Must trees fall only on the heads of common people? Why not on the heads of queens? Well, leave that aside. Shall we go up to the palanquin now and speak to the Ilaiya Rani? Shall we request her help in getting into the Thanjavur fort?'

'Wonderful idea! You couldn't have picked a better time to seek an audience with the Ilaiya Rani! Or a better place! If we approach the palanquin, they will mistake us for bandits and beat us up!'

'If I see the Ilaiya Rani, things will get easier.'

'How?'

'I'll mention my Anni's name, or I'll tell her Ravidasan sent me.'

'Good idea, but how will you do it unless you get close? … Look there, Poonguzhali!'

There was yet another flash of lightning. And they saw two men carrying the palanquin. Were they leaving, then? No, no … the palanquin appeared to be headed for the mandapam!

Soon enough, the palanquin entered the mandapam. The two men set it down.

'The Pazhuvoor Ilaiya Rani has come in search of us!' Poonguzhali said.

Senthan Amudan took her hand to usher her into the inner recesses of the mandapam, but she stood firm.

'Who goes there?' a voice boomed.

Poonguzhali realised it belonged to one of the palanquin bearers and called, 'Don't worry, Anna! We're wayfarers like you. We're taking shelter from the rain here.'

'All right, all right. Don't come close to the palanquin,' the same voice said.

'Why would we come close to the palanquin? How could we have earned the privilege of riding a palanquin?' Poonguzhali said.

'Tiruvalluvar has spoken about this too,' Senthan Amudan said. 'While speaking of how the good deeds of one birth pay in ...'

'Enough, enough! Shut up now! How many of you are there?'

'There are only two of us. There is enough space in the mandapam to hold another two hundred,' Senthan Amudan said.

When he gave them the count, he was not aware of a third person hiding behind a pillar in the mandapam.

'I told you back then, we should go and take shelter in the mandapam. No one listened to me. That's why we're in trouble now!' the palanquin bearer told his companion.

'Who thought something like this would happen? We wanted to hurry into the fort before the rain intensified. At least the tree didn't fall on the palanquin!' the other man said.

At that moment, there was another flash of lightning. Senthan Amudan and Poonguzhali had their eyes and attention fixed on the palanquin, and so they saw a woman part the curtains from within and stare at them. They also saw her smile at them in recognition.

The next moment, the mandapam was in darkness.

'Amuda, did you see?' Poonguzhali whispered.

'I did.'

'Who was in the palanquin?'

'The Pazhuvoor Ilaiya Rani, no?'

'What did you think?'

'It did look like her. But then, I had a little doubt.'

'No doubt. It's certain.'

'What is?'

'It's not the Pazhuvoor Rani. It's my crazy Aththai Rani who is in the palanquin!'

'Sssh! Don't talk!'

'If I don't talk, how will it happen?'

'How will what happen?'

'What we came all this way to do. We've found Aththai. Now, we must free her and take her with us, no?'

'That's impossible, Poonguzhali! We'll see where the palanquin goes. And then we'll think of a way to free her.'

'So you're suggesting we let go of the elephant's trunk and grab the tail? No, I can't do all that. We must free Aththai right away. If you're scared, you don't have to do anything!'

'Your Aththai must consent to being freed, no? She's being escorted with pomp and ceremony in a palanquin. Where is she going? Why? And at whose instance? Shouldn't we find out first?'

'What if they're taking her to the dungeon? What would we do about it if we wait until then? We can't get her out from there!'

'Why not? I was there myself and I got out. I too have some influence in royal palaces. I'll rescue your Aththai one way or another. Now, be quiet!'

Poonguzhali decided it would be most prudent to be quiet.

But then, something happened that neither expected.

The screen that had parted slightly now seemed to part further. A figure slipped out from within. Without making the slightest sound, she walked away from it like a cat. The next moment, she was right by their side. Since all this happened in pitch dark, the two men who stood guard at the front steps of the mandapam did not notice a thing.

Poonguzhali could tell that the woman who had got out of the palanquin was her Aththai despite the darkness. The Oomai Rani took their hands and ushered them quietly to the interior of the mandapam.

She embraced Poonguzhali and kissed the top of her head, to show her how happy she was to see her niece. Then, aunt and niece had a conversation through hand gestures. How did they see each other? How could each tell what the other was saying? We can't quite explain that.

Poonguzhali turned to Senthan Amudan and asked, 'Could you make out what Aththai was saying? She asked me to get into the palanquin in her place. She wants you to take her to your house.'

'And what do you want to do?'

'I'm going to do as Aththai says. Isn't that the best ploy to find out who gave orders for her capture?'

'Think before you consent, Poonguzhali. It might be the best ploy, but it could put you in peril.'

'Amuda, don't worry! Doing as Aththai said won't put me in peril. And if I find myself in danger, I have a dagger with me right here!' Poonguzhali said.

She embraced her aunt once more, and then went as quietly towards the palanquin as the Oomai Rani had walked away from it. She entered the palanquin and drew the screen closed.

22

ANIRUDDHAR, BETRAYED

Prime Minister Aniruddha Brahmarayar had been in the capital for some days. Government officials, suzerain kings, army generals, messengers from other lands, representatives of traders' groups, scholars of the southern and northern languages, and temple administrators sought audiences with him. His palace was bustling with activity and brimming with people.

Aniruddhar had chosen not to have a dedicated security detail for himself. His entourage was small. And so, there was no reason for the Pazhuvettaraiyars to take issue with him.

And yet, Chinna Pazhuvettaraiyar muttered away to himself. Ever since the prime minister had stepped into the fort, the security had become more lax. Anyone who claimed to have an appointment with the prime minister was allowed to enter. The prime minister's palace was right next to the emperor's, and the crowd that was waiting to meet him spilled onto the courtyard of the royal palace as well. Several people arrived with Aniruddha Brahmarayar's seal, which permitted them to meet the prime minister.

Chinna Pazhuvettaraiyar wanted to curtail these face-to-face meetings, but he lacked the courage to confront the prime minister. If only his elder brother had been there, the two of them could have put their heads together and come up with a solution. But Periya Pazhuvettaraiyar had chosen this time of all times to go to Kadambur. Kalantaka Kandar felt as if he had lost the use of an arm.

As if it was not enough that he had caused the entire town to enter the fort and put its security at peril, Aniruddhar had also got into the habit of sending Chinna Pazhuvettaraiyar orders in the guise of requests.

Some days earlier, he had asked for some soldiers because he wanted to send them to Kodikkarai. Chinna Pazhuvettaraiyar sent them along. Then, the previous day, the prime minister had said a woman from a noble family had to be escorted from Thiruvaiyaaru and asked if he might have use of the Pazhuvoor palace's closed palanquin and some bearers to carry it. Chinna Pazhuvettaraiyar fulfilled the request.

However, he had a feeling that the prime minister was planning something devious. Who was the woman, and from which noble family? Why was she coming here? He simply had to find out. What a time for his brother to be held up elsewhere!

There was another man who was keen to find out the identity of the occupant of the palanquin being escorted to the prime minister's palace. He was none other than Aniruddha Brahmarayar's premier disciple, Azhvarkadiyaan.

On the morning following the downpour, once the prime minister finished his ritual bath, prayers and punaskaram[1], he made his way to the palace courtyard. He sent a servant to check who was waiting for an audience with him. When he was told that Azhvarkadiyaan was among them, he sent for his disciple right away.

Azhvarkadiyaan stood humbly before his preceptor, his hands folded in devotion.

'Tirumalai! What became of your mission?' Aniruddhar asked.

'Guru! Please forgive me. I have failed,' Azhvarkadiyaan said.

'That isn't unexpected. Were you not able to meet Aditya Karikalar at all?'

'I did, aiya! I passed on your message, but it was of no use. I wasn't able to stop the prince from going to the Kadambur palace.'

'So, is the prince in Kadambur right now?'

'Yes, my guru! I saw him enter Sambuvarayar's palace. The prince was given a royal reception. The excitement of the people defies description.'

'That is to be expected. Who else has arrived at the palace?'

'Parthibendran and Vandiyadevan accompanied the prince. Periya Pazhuvettaraiyar went from here, with the Ilaiya Rani. I heard that several suzerain kings from Nadu Naadu and Tirumunaippadi have been invited.'

'Tirukkovalur Malayaman ...?'

'He rode with the prince up to the Manimuththa river and then returned.'

'The old soldier will not stay quiet. He must be busy gathering an army now. I've had news from the south that Kodumbalur Periya Velaan is marching here with an enormous army. Only God can ensure that no harm comes to the rajyam! Tirumalai ... what were the people of Chozha Naadu talking about? Did you overhear anything on your way, anything that would tell us what occupies their thoughts?'

'The conversation was largely about the accident that has befallen the younger prince. They are furious with the Pazhuvettaraiyar brothers. Some blame you as well ...'

'True, true, they are justified. Tirumalai! I plan to resign from my post soon.'

'O guru! If you were to do that, I would regain my freedom too. I could travel through the land, singing the paasurams of the Azhvars and live in bliss. When do you intend to resign, aiya?'

'I'm going to make one last attempt to protect the rajyam from harm. Once that's done, I will resign.'

'And what does that attempt involve?'

'The first and most important step has already been completed. Tirumalai! I've succeeded in a task on which you gave up, claiming it was impossible!'

'That is no surprise, aiya. But, pray, what is this task?'

'I asked you to find a deaf-mute woman who wanders like a lunatic through the islands of Eezham and bring her here, didn't I? And you returned saying you were not able to accomplish this task, didn't you?'

'Yes, aiya! That deaf-mute woman …'

'… has been brought to the palace as of last night.'

'Aha! What a wonder! How did you achieve this?'

'I expected that woman to come to Kodikkarai to find out whether the prince had escaped with his life. I had sent men to capture her and bring her here if she was spotted. Thankfully, she came without resisting much. Tirumalai, would you believe I had her carried from Thiruvaiyaaru in a closed palanquin, and that the palanquin I sent was the Pazhuvoor Ilaiya Rani's?'

'Aiya, there was a storm last night, wasn't there?'

'Yes. And that proved an obstacle on the way. I was worried too. It was only when the palanquin arrived here in the middle of the night that I could breathe.'

'Oho! It was the middle of the night, was it? And you stayed up to receive her?'

'I was awake, but I did not go to receive her. I had the women of the house welcome her. Who knows how a lunatic might react to any reception? I was worried. But, thankfully, there was no trouble.

She ate her fill and then slept right away. Tirumalai! To be honest, I'm somewhat scared to meet her. I'm glad you arrived when you did.'

'O guru! I'm very, very keen to meet that woman.'

'In that case, come along. Let us go to the antapuram. She knows you already, doesn't she? And she knows you are a friend of the prince's. It is likely that she will be more at ease in your presence.'

The preceptor and the disciple went to the antapuram, where the prime minister bade the maids usher her in.

They did as they had been told.

Aniruddhar looked at the woman and jumped out of his skin.

A smile danced on Azhvarkadiyaan's lips.

23

CAN THE MUTE SPEAK?

Aniruddhar stared at Poonguzhali for some time, and then gestured to the maids who had ushered her in, calling them aside. He asked them something in a soft voice. Once he had got their response, he asked them to leave the room.

He then turned to Azhvarkadiyaan and asked, 'Tirumalai! There appears to have been a mistake.'

'True, aiya. I feel the same way.'

'This is a young woman. She can't be over twenty years old.'

'Not even twenty, I would think.'

'The lady I was expecting must be around forty.'

'No, older.'

'Yes, yes, you've seen Mandakini Devi in Lanka, haven't you?'

'Yes, aiya. I saw her and—in accordance with your orders—attempted to bring her back here, but failed in the mission.'

'This woman is not Mandakini Devi, is she?'

'No, gurudevare! She is certainly not Mandakini ammaiyar.'

'Then, who could she be? How has she landed up here?'

'We might as well ask her,' Azhvarkadiyaan said.

'What is the point of asking someone who is mute?'

'Gurudevare ... it hasn't been ascertained that she is mute, has it?'

'I was asking the maids. They said she hasn't spoken a word since she arrived.'

'Gurudevare, whom did you send to identify her and bring her to you?'

'Aha! Has that fool made a mistake?'

'Which fool, gurudevare? Surely, you could not have entrusted such a task to a fool?'

'He appeared intelligent. The day I went to Pazhaiyarai, a young man was fighting with Vandiyadevan, remember?'

'Yes, the son of the physician, Pinagapani.'

'Yes, he's the one. Once I had despatched you and Vandiyadevan to intercept Aditya Karikalar, I freed that physician's son from the prison and gauged that he would make a good addition to our army of spies. I sent him to Kodikkarai. He said he had been there before often, and knew the place well.'

'Was he the one who brought this woman here?'

'I gave him all the right identifiers. And he sent word from Thiruvaiyaaru that the mission had been successful.'

'Aiya! Where is that intelligent spy who has succeeded in the mission at which I failed? It would be a good idea to ask him about this lady, wouldn't it?'

'True, but he was involved in an unforeseen, unfortunate accident last night.'

'Adada! What accident, what happened?'

'He was following the palanquin. In accordance with my instructions that they should enter the fortress after dark, he left at dusk from Thiruvaiyaaru and was nearing the fort by night. The storm took them by surprise, as you know ...'

'Yes, aiya. I took shelter in a mandapam for yatris by the side of the road.'

'As the palanquin was approaching the fort, a large tree fell by the roots across the road. Thankfully, it didn't fall on the palanquin, but it did fall on the people coming right behind. Pinagapani was trapped under the tree.'

The prime minister had no sooner spoken the words than he heard a woman's voice say, 'Why did the tree alone fall on that sandaalan's head? Why wasn't he also struck by a bolt of lightning?'

Aniruddhar, startled by the rage in the voice, turned to see who had spoken. His mouth fell open when he realised the speaker was Poonguzhali. Without taking his eyes off her, he asked, 'Tirumalai, was it this girl who spoke just now?'

'Yes, aiya, so it seems.'

'What wonder is this? Can the deaf hear? Can the mute speak?'

'It would indeed be a wonder if the deaf could hear and the mute could speak. But if such a pious devotee of Lord Vishnu, the Omnipotent One, as yourself were to wish for it, why shouldn't a miracle occur? The Azhvars have graced us with the words ...'

'Enough! Don't irritate me by dragging the Azhvars into this. This is not the fruit of Lord Vishnu's compassion, but an error of some sort. This woman has tricked us. Who is she? What are her intentions? Why has she been acting deaf-mute all this while?'

'Gurudevare! We might as well ask the lady herself.'

'Appane, the smile on your face suggests you might know the answer yourself. All right, as you wish! I will ask the lady herself. Penne! Are you not deaf? Can you hear my words?'

'Aiya! There are times when I have wished I were deaf. But I am now happy that I am not. How else would I have heard the news that a tree fell on the head of the physician's son? Swami, is he dead and gone?'

'Aha! You can hear. And you speak too. You're not mute!' Aniruddhar said.

'This girl is certainly not mute,' his disciple said.

'Aha! You've divined that I'm not mute. So what I've heard is true ... that the most intelligent, the wisest man in the Chozha empire is the prime minister, Aniruddha Brahmarayar!' Poonguzhali said.

'Penne! You mock me, do you? Careful! If you're not mute, why have you not spoken a word since you arrived? Why were you pretending to be deaf-mute? Tell me the truth!' the prime minister commanded.

'Aiya, until I arrived here last night, I did have a tendency to talk. People have even called me "vaayaadi" because I can't keep my mouth shut. But when I saw the honourable prime minister's palace and was given a royal reception upon entering, I was literally struck dumb. The women of your palace spoke to me through gestures. I figured they were all mute, and so I responded through gestures too. But after hearing you speak, I remembered that I can speak as well ...'

'There's no doubt that you're a vaayaadi. I'm surprised the physician's son was able to capture you. He might be a fool, but he's enterprising.'

'Swami, that moron did not capture me. If he had so much as tried, he would have been on a yatra to Yamalokam by now!' Poonguzhali said, brandishing the knife tucked into her waistband.

'Penne! A thousand blessings on you, please put that knife away. Why are you so angry with him? You just said he did not capture you.'

'He did not capture me. But his men tied me to my boat. They tied my Anni to a tree. And on top of everything else, that sandaala physician's son told me he had nothing to do with all this.'

'He's done well on that count. He did and spoke as I asked.'

'Aiya! O Prime Minister! Was it you who sent that rakshasa? Was it you who also ordered that my deaf-mute Aththai be captured and brought here?'

'Your Aththai? The daughter of the karaiyar, Mandakini Devi, is your Aththai? In that case ... you must be related to the lighthouse keeper at Kalangarai, Tyagavidangar?'

'Aiya, I am his daughter.'

'Aha! I didn't realise that Tyagavidangar had such a chatterbox of a daughter!'

'Please keep that to yourself, aiya.'

'Why, penne?'

'They say nothing happens in the Chozha empire without the prime minister hearing of it. If the people were to learn that you didn't realise my father had such a chatterbox of a daughter, their respect for and awe of you might be diminished, don't you think?'

'Penne, I'm not worried about respect and awe. Please tell me one other thing I don't know. You said they had captured your Aththai. Where is she now? How did you get on the palanquin I had sent? Where did you mount it?' Aniruddhar asked.

'Aiya! Why did you send soldiers to capture my deaf-mute, helpless Aththai?'

'Magale, I cannot disclose that to you. That is a secret, with royal connections.'

'Thanthaiye! In that case, I cannot answer your question either.'

'There are ways to make you answer.'

'Those won't work on me.'

'Penne! I will have you held in the dungeon.'

'No dungeon can hold me.'

'People who are sent to the dungeon never return.'

'I know someone who has, aiya. In fact, I was talking to Senthan Amudan on my way here. We journeyed together.'

'Who is that, Senthan Amudan?'

'He is my other Aththai's son. The two of us came from Kodikkarai.'

'Why, magale?'

'I have always wanted to see the terraced mansions and layered gopurams of Thanjavur. And I wanted a darshan of the emperor. They say Sundara Chozha Chakravarti is unwell. How is he now, aiya? May I see him?'

'He is just as he was before, magale. There has been no progress. So, please forget about getting a darshan ...'

'How can I forget, aiya? I must absolutely meet the emperor. I must tell him of the crimes against women that are happening here, how women are being kidnapped in his dharmarajyam ...'

'Penne! I don't have the time to engage in a pointless debate with you. I did not give orders to force you here. Tell me how you came to be in the palanquin I had sent. Did someone force you into it?'

'No, swami, that did not happen. When I was nearing the Thanjai fort, I saw that the palanquin was empty. Since it was raining, I decided to get inside it.'

The prime minister turned to his disciple and said, 'I have more or less understood what happened. They must have set the palanquin down somewhere to shelter from the rain. This girl would have swapped places with her Aththai at that time. Because the physician's son was trapped under the tree, he wasn't there to spot it. The guards and palanquin bearers were not paying close attention. This must have happened quite close to the palace, Tirumalai. Do you think I'm right?'

'Swami. It is exactly as you said. I was an eyewitness.'

'You were? How? Why? Why were you silent all this while? Tell me quickly, now!'

'I was nearing the fort last evening, when it began to rain. There was a downpour, which turned into a thunderstorm in no time. Trees were uprooted. I decided to take shelter at a mandapam off the road, built for travellers. Not long after I reached one, this girl came there with a young man. He must be the cousin she mentioned just now. I saw rudraksha beads around his neck when the lightning pierced the darkness. Realising he had been indoctrinated with Shaivism from infancy, I decided to speak to him about the greatness of Vaishnavism. It would keep me entertained, I thought. Just then, more people arrived at the mandapam and set down a palanquin. The palm tree symbol of the Pazhuvettaraiyar clan was visible on the screen. A woman got down from the palanquin and approached these two. The three of them went to a dark corner of the mandapam and spoke in gestures. Then, I saw this girl enter the palanquin. There was another flash of lightning just then, which allowed me to ascertain that she was not the woman who had got down from the palanquin. The palanquin bearers did not notice any of this. Once the rain let up, they lifted the palanquin and went their way.'

'Aha! So they have tricked me! And you kept quiet about all this! What did the other two do after that?'

'They left once the palanquin had been carried away. And I left too.'

'Tirumalai! Why did you choose to be a silent witness to all this? Why didn't you stop her Aththai from getting out? Are you in cahoots with them?'

'What a thing to say, gurudevare! Abachaaram, abachaaram! I am not capable of such betrayal! First, I did not know you were the architect of this plan. Having seen the palm tree symbol on the palanquin, I figured it was Chinna Pazhuvettaraiyar's order that had been carried out. Besides, do you think I can stop Mandakini Devi? Dams might help contain the damage caused by storms, but can anyone contain that queen among women? I attempted and failed in Lanka.

Besides, she knows who I am. If she had spotted me, she would have run away. Then, no one would have been able to find her …'

'This is why it appears the physician's son is rather clever. He did bring her up to this point, didn't he?'

'Gurudevare! I'm afraid you're mistaken on that count. Mandakini Devi must have come of her own free will. She must have changed her mind upon reaching Thanjai.'

'Perhaps. Perhaps. But she could not have gone far. It was raining all night, wasn't it? She must be somewhere nearby. Tirumalai! We must capture her somehow. Perhaps this girl knows where we might find her … magale! What is your name?'

'Poonguzhali, aiya.'

'Aha! What a lovely name! Your father has no match in this department. Poonguzhali! You must know where your aunt is taking shelter. If you do know, please tell us. No harm will come to her.'

Poonguzhali thought for a while and said, 'Swami, I know where my Aththai is staying. If you tell me why you want her brought here, I'll tell you where she is.'

'Poonguzhali, that is a royal matter. You cannot be let in on palace secrets.'

'Then, you cannot be let in on the location of her hideout.'

'There is no point speaking to this girl.'

'Aiya, if you agree to a condition …'

'Aha! This girl is laying out conditions for me, is she? What might that condition be, pray?'

'If you will seat my Aththai on the throne of Thanjavur and place a bejewelled crown on her head, I'll bring her here myself.'

'Tirumalai! This girl has gone insane!'

'Have you only just realised this, gurudevare? You need not ask her anything. I know where her Aththai is. Her cousin's home is in a garden, some distance from the fort. He and his mother are in charge of the flower decorations at the Talikulaththaar temple. That is where you will find Mandakini Devi. If you send some men with me, I'll bring her here,' Azhvarkadiyaan said.

Poonguzhali glared at Azhvarkadiyaan as if she would burn him to ashes and said, 'If you do anything of the sort, I will go stand before the emperor's palace right now and demand justice! I will tell the entire world of the atrocities you have committed!'

'Tirumalai! We must send her to the dungeon right away. There is no other option,' Aniruddha Brahmarayar said.

'I will kill anyone who comes near me!' Poonguzhali said, brandishing her knife.

'Aiya, there is no need to send this girl to the dungeon. Let us send her to Ilaiya Piraatti Kundavai Devi's palace instead. The princess is here now, isn't she? She will cure this girl of her insanity. Perhaps

Ilaiya Piraatti will have some use for this girl too,' Azhvarkadiyaan said.

'What makes you say that? What use could the Ilaiya Piraatti have for this girl?'

'Gurudevare! Don't you know? The thunderstorm that hit us last evening has caused devastation along the coast. Messengers from everywhere are waiting for you outside your palace.'

'Yes, yes, I must meet them all now. I've wasted enough time on this girl. If only she had been born mute too ...'

'When there is no law and order, no dispensation of justice, it is torment, isn't it ...' Poonguzhali muttered to herself.

'I have heard that Nagapattinam is in great danger. They say a tidal wave swept over the entire town and swallowed it whole ...'

This statement drew a gasp from both Aniruddhar and Poonguzhali.

'The princess herself might come here to speak to you about it,' Azhvarkadiyaan said.

He had barely finished speaking when cheers and cries of joy were heard from the courtyard.

'Tirumalai, since when have you been gifted gnana drishti? It appears Ilaiya Piraatti is here!' Aniruddhar said, getting up and making for the palace gates.

Before he could get there, Kundavai Devi and Vanathi entered the palace.

When Ilaiya Piraatti saw Poonguzhali standing there, the look of anxiety on her face was replaced by one of surprise and delight in equal measure.

The story continues in

BOOK 8

VENGEANT SON

An Extract

COMMOTION IN KADAMBUR

Ever since Aditya Karikalan had set foot in the Kadambur palace, the residents and guests had been forced to spend their time standing as if on thorns and walking as if on fire. No one could tell what kind of weapon would issue from the prince's mouth at any given time. And so, everyone was in torment.

Karikalan often made snide references to the conspiracy to seat Madurantakan on the Chozha throne. Pazhuvettaraiyar couldn't bear this. He met Sambuvarayar and tried to convince him that they should openly tell the prince about the suzerain kings' opinions.

'Please hold on,' Sambuvarayar said. 'Just be patient a little while longer. He has arrived as our guest. And he's behaving like a raging bull. What if things take a completely unforeseen turn? We must be prudent until the time is right to tell him.'

The conversation kept getting postponed.

Eventually, Aditya Karikalan spared them the trouble by bringing it up himself in the presence of everyone at the palace.

'I have come here to seek the opinion of Pazhuvoor Paattan and Kadambur Maaman[1] on an important matter. I'll ask you now. Three years ago, my father made me the crown prince of the Chozha empire. All of you gave your consent at the time. Now, I hear the emperor has changed his opinion. I believe he wishes to crown Madurantakan in my place. This is why he has been sending me invitation upon invitation to come to Thanjavur. And I've been postponing my visit. Why should I go to Thanjavur? Why should I go and disobey my father to his face? Isn't it better that I refrain from going? Pazhuvoor Paattaa! Kadambur Maamaa! You are elders. You are aware of what is right and what is wrong, of dharma and justice and fairness. You tell me. Is it fair of my father to ask me to give up my title for Madurantakan? And if I refuse to do so, would it be wrong?' Aditya Karikalan asked.

Everyone was stunned.

Pazhuvettaraiyar cleared his throat and tried to deflect the question with, 'Komagane! You must have asked your Tirukkovalur Paattan his opinion. What did Malayaman have to say?'

'Aha! Surely you know the old man's nature? Do you think he would consent to his grandson giving up the throne for someone else? He would rather kill me and the mother who birthed me than allow it! Malayaman has begun to gather an army, to assert his grandson's right to the throne. But I am not going to listen to him alone. Whatever all of you say, I will go with it,' Karikalan said, like an obedient child.

Fooled by his tone, Pazhuvettaraiyar said, 'We're not going to incite a son to go against his father like Malayaman has. Whatever the emperor's wishes and orders are, we are bound to follow them. But we do have the right to an opinion on what is just and fair. It cannot be said that the emperor's argument is without grounding. It cannot be said that Madurantaka Devar has no claim on the Chozha empire. Ilavarase! If it is your wish that we speak openly, we will. The decision is yours. It would be dangerous to let the difference of opinion grow any further. So, it would be prudent to arrive at a compromise. The Chozha empire is not restricted to the area between the two Vellaaru rivers as it was before. It stretches between Kumari Munai and the Krishna river. Even if it were split into two, each half would be a mighty empire in itself. It is our opinion that we should give the portion of the empire that is south of the Kollidam river to Madurantaka Devar, and the portion to the north to you. If you're in agreement with this, we can take the next steps. I will take upon myself the responsibility of convincing the empire to consent to this arrangement.'

Aditya Karikalan burst into laughter.

Periya Pazhuvettaraiyar felt as if his stomach was on fire.

'Paattaa!' Aditya Karikalan said. 'It is certainly a fair division of the Chozha empire, for the Pazhuvettaraiyars to rule the south and the Sambuvarayars to rule the north, a fitting reward for the service your two clans have rendered the crown since the time of my great-grandfather. But I have no interest in splitting the empire. To share an empire that has been passed down through the generations is akin to sharing one's wedded wife. Old men like you might be happy with such an arrangement, but I am not!'

Sparks flew from Pazhuvettaraiyar's eyes. He rose, furious, and was ready to draw his sword from the scabbard.

'Paattaa! You're already leaving? Please hear me out before you go! I do not consent to splitting the empire. It has grown from the toils of my ancestors and yours, going back five generations. We have fought wars, and countless warriors have sacrificed their lives in service of this empire. It would be a sin to split it into two little kingdoms. Our ancestors, including Rajadityar who attained Heaven as a hero, will curse us for this act. So let go of that thought. I am willing to give up the entire empire for Madurantakan. And it would be justified too. He is the son of my great-uncle. He should have been seated on the throne in my father's stead. It was because of Parantaka Chakravarti's plans that my father was crowned king. Let that wrong die with him. Going by the laws of inheritance, I have every right to claim the throne after him, but I am willing to give it up. But I have one condition. I need an army with 3,00,000 soldiers to march on the lands to the north. The supplies and equipment this army needs as well as food provisions for a year must be arranged. I also need 300 warships that are capable of navigating the high seas. I intend to appoint Parthibendran the commander of the navy. He will arrive by sea, while I march on land. We will meet at the mouth of the Ganga river and march further north. The poets have sung that my ancestor, the one whose name I bear, Karikal Valavan, raised the tiger flag on the Himalayas. I will emulate his achievement. On the strength of my sword and on the strength of the shoulders of the warriors who accompany me, I will conquer the lands north of the Krishna river and become emperor of lands I have claimed for myself. And if I taste defeat in place of triumph, if I am killed in battle, I will die happy for having proven that the Chozhas are a valorous clan and join my ancestors in the warriors' heaven. Pazhuvoor Paattaa! Kadambur Maamaa! What do you say? Do you agree to fulfil this condition?'

Having spoken with such authority, Karikalan fell silent.

The two old men were stunned.

Pazhuvettaraiyar stammered, 'Ilavarase! Who are we to fulfil your conditions? What right do we have? You must ask the emperor, not us!'

At this, Karikalan rose in rage and roared, 'Paattaa! Who do you think you can fool by invoking the emperor's name? Not me! I will not be fooled! You have imprisoned my father in your palace and have made him a puppet whose strings you pull! Did you think I was not aware of this? Can anyone meet my father without Chinna Pazhuvettaraiyar's permission? Was the letter ordering the arrest of my brother and his return from Eezham written of my father's free will? Or because of your coercion? Would any father write that the nation's beloved prince, dearer to them than their own eyes, his youngest child, the bravest of warriors, should be imprisoned and escorted home? The entire kingdom is blazing with fury at you for imprisoning Arulmozhi and killing him by sinking the ship in which he was being brought home …'

'Ilavarase! Who dared speak such a terrible untruth? I will shred his tongue and then cut him into pieces!' Periya Pazhuvettaraiyar hollered.

'You could do that if it was a single person. But it is ten thousand, a hundred thousand, a million people. If you were to punish all of them, Chozha Naadu would turn into a mound of corpses, an open graveyard, a field of pyres! Why, that would be the ideal setting for the epitome of Shiva bhakti, Madurantaka Devan, to rule! But, Paattaa, I don't believe that. People are fools. They repeat a tall tale one person comes up with, not stopping to analyse it for logic. You, who have been traditional supporters and well-wishers of the Chozha clan, could never have stooped to such a terrible deed. If Arulmozhi has drowned at sea, it is his fate. It must have been his destiny to show up the astrologers and palmists who predicted that he had been born to rule the three worlds. Paattaa! However courageous a warrior you have been, however skilled a commander, you could not possibly have conjured a storm at sea or caused a thunderbolt to fall on the mast of the ship. Perhaps that was an act of the mantravadis of Pandiya Naadu. You are not responsible for that. And, therefore, you are not responsible for Arulmozhi's death either. But please don't tell me you need to ask the emperor's permission for anything. Next, you'll tell me you'll have to run it by that Anbil Brahmarayan. The emperor and the prime minister have nominal titles. They cannot do anything that goes against your wishes. Perhaps you can tell me you will need to check with Pazhuvoor Paatti Nandini Devi …'

At this, Kandamaaran intervened and stammered something along the lines of, 'Aiya! People who have been invited as guests to our home …'

Aditya Karikalan turned in his direction, his eyes spitting fire, and laughed like Shiva after he had burned the three fortresses of iron, silver and gold that the sons of the asura Taruka had got as a boon from Brahma. He then said, 'Kandamaaran! This is your home, is it? I forgot! I also forgot that you come from the dynasty of Valvil Ori of Kollimalai! What a brave clan that is! Well, one must be careful what one says in your home, particularly in your presence. What have I said that was wrong? What have I done to the people who have been invited as guests to your home?

Kandamaaran! Why are your arms and legs trembling? Has the fever that spread throughout Eezham affected you too? Even though you didn't go to Eezham?'

Vandiyadevan said, 'Komagane! Kandamaaran is not affected by the fever. He is angry that you referred to the Pazhuvoor Ilaiya Rani as "Paatti"!'

Kandamaaran glared at Vandiyadevan and reached for his dagger. Parthibendran stopped his hand and forced him to sit down. He whispered something into Kandamaaran's ear, which appeared to calm the latter down. But Kandamaaran's body continued to shake.

Karikalan looked at him, laughed and then turned to Pazhuvettaraiyar. 'Paatta! This is the nature of young bulls. They sometimes frisk about, refusing to stay contained in their sheds. Don't worry about them. If you are my grandfather, Ilaiya Rani is my grandmother, isn't she? When I call you "Paattaa", I must call her "Paatti"! My Paatti is not troubled by it. Neither are you. Why are these little boys so angry about it? Well, it doesn't matter. I've meandered from what I was saying. Please do not place the burden on my father, the emperor. If you consent to my condition, it is as good as my father's consent. You have control of the treasury. If I announce that I intend to march on the north, I will find not 3,00,000 but three million soldiers to volunteer. It won't be hard to gather 300 ships either. I need your consent and that of Madurantaka Devan. That's all. What do you say?'

Pazhuvettaraiyar stumbled and stammered and hemmed and hawed before he cleared his throat and said, 'Komagane! Even if I were to consent to this entirely unexpected condition of yours, we need Madurantakar's consent, don't we? And surely you will not wage a war without taking leave of the emperor? So, let us all go to Thanjavur and ...'

'No, that alone is impossible. Paattaa, if my father gives me some other order when I am in Thanjavur, I will not be able to flout it. Besides, my mother, the daughter of Malayaman, is there. My sister Ilaiya Piraatti is there too. They will not approve of my renouncing the crown and wandering the world as an ascetic in warrior's guise. Paattaa! This matter must be decided right here, in the Kadambur Palace. Please go to Thanjavur yourself and bring Madurantakan here. Once we have spoken amongst ourselves, we can convey our decision to my father. And when all the arrangements have been made for the army to march, I will go to Thanjavur and take leave of my parents. Or, my parents can crown Madurantakan emperor right away and come to Kanchi. I will settle them into the golden palace I have built for them, and then leave for war.'

Pazhuvettaraiyar turned to Sambuvarayar. Sambuvarayar was staring at the ceiling. Realising that no help would be forthcoming from his host, Pazhuvettaraiyar said, 'Komagane! What can I do but obey your orders?'

'Do not call them "orders", Paattaa! How can a mere boy such as I issue orders to you, whose hair has greyed in service to the crown of Chozha Naadu? You will be fulfilling my petition, that's all,' Aditya Karikalan said.

'As you wish,' Pazhuvettaraiyar said, and cleared his throat again.

'I am ever grateful to you, Paattaa! Please do make arrangements to leave as soon as you can. And please bring Madurantakan to Kadambur on elephant back, for all to see. Let him not travel in Ilaiya Paatti's palanquin this time!' Aditya Karikalan said, with a laugh.

Then, he turned to Kandamaaran and the others and said, 'Kandamaara! Look at your good fortune! There will be more guests in your home! The man who will be emperor after Sundara Chozhar, Madurantakar, is coming to your home. There's also a chance that his queen, Chinna Pazhuvettaraiyar's daughter, will grace your home. The Kadambur palace will be a site of great celebration! Let Pazhuvoor Paattanaar leave for Thanjai. And let *us* leave on a hunt! Come, let's go! I was once a skilled archer. People used to say, "Aditya Karikalan is second only to Arjuna." But I have not so much as held a bow in three years, and I have forgotten archery. I must practise again. Parthibendra! Vandiyadeva! Get ready, let's all leave! Where shall we go to hunt? Kollimalai, perhaps?'

Sambuvarayar, who had been silent all this while, said, 'Komagane! Kollimalai is a great distance away. You needn't travel so far to hunt. To the west of the Veeranarayana lake is a dense forest. We call it the "Dhandakaranyam". You will find plenty of game there. The mounts you see in our trophy hall are all animals that were hunted in the Dhandakaranyam. It is close to the palace. If you leave in the morning, you can return by dusk!'

'Then that's what we'll do, aiya. For as long as I am a guest at this palace, your word is law to me. May we take your daughter Manimeghalai along on the hunt? She has a way of spreading cheer and joy wherever she goes!' Aditya Karikalan said.

'I have no objection,' Sambuvarayar said. 'Let us ask Manimeghalai.'

Kandamaaran said, 'What place do women have on a hunt? We will constantly be preoccupied with their safety. How can we focus on the hunt? Besides, Nandini Devi needs a companion here.'

'Of course, of course. Kandamaaran is always worried about Pazhuvoor Paatti alone. Well, there is another problem with taking Manimeghalai along. She's always skipping along and leaping about. What if someone mistakes her for a deer and aims an arrow at her? Let the women remain in the palace. We will go by ourselves. We must leave at dawn. The kuravai koothu must finish early tonight, and everyone must go rest right away. Make sure you get your sleep. Aiya!

Please tell all the hunters to do this. Vandiyadeva! Come, let us repair to our quarters!'

With that, Aditya Karikalan took Vandiyadevan by the arm and hurried off. Kandamaaran and Parthibendran looked on as they disappeared, not without envy. Sambuvarayar went to speak to the hunters. Pazhuvettaraiyar went to the antapuram in search of Nandini.

NOTES

1. BY THE BANKS OF THE KEDILAM

1. The more popular spelling of this river is 'Gadilam', just as the more popular spelling of 'Kandaradityar' is 'Gandaradityar'. However, I have chosen to stay more faithful to the Tamil spellings.
2. Appar had, for a time, converted to Jainism, and become a revered leader known as 'Dharmasena'. His sister, who had remained a Shaivite, prayed to Lord Shiva to lead her brother back to Shaivism. Soon after, Appar got afflicted with a severe stomach pain that had left him writhing. His sister had spread sacred ash on his forehead, asked him to pray to Lord Shiva and led him to the temple in this town. There he is said to have recited his first padigam, which mollified Shiva enough to cure Appar and bestow the epithet 'Tirunavukkarasar' on him, in which 'tiru' means 'honourable', 'navu' means 'tongue' and 'arasar' means 'king'.
3. This simple sentence contains much context. Tamil mythology speaks of eight places where Shiva appeared before his devotees or enemies in disguise to test or kill

them, as the case may be. These eight places were then named 'veerattaanam'. Tiruvadigai is known as the site of the Tripura Samhara—when Shiva killed three asuras named Vidyunmali, Tarukakshan and Kamalakshan who lived in palaces of gold, silver and iron. These palaces were empowered to fly, thus enabling the asuras to torment mortals and devas.

4. One of the padigams sung by Sundaramurti refers to an incident at this spot. Sundaramurti was resting at the Tirunavalur temple, when he felt someone kicking at his legs. Assuming it was a devotee wanting more place, he moved slightly, only for someone to start kicking his head. When he woke up in irritation, he saw that the offender was Lord Shiva. Sundaramurti apparently wept for joy and wrote a poem right away to commemorate the incident.
5. An immortal.

2. GRANDFATHER AND GRANDSON

1. 'Kuzhandai' means 'child', and usually refers to an infant or a very young child. When used for adults, it is used as an endearment, usually only by older relatives and very occasionally by close family friends. 'Kuzhandaai' is one of the forms that can be used while calling the addressee.
2. Modern-day Malkheda.
3. The mythological flood that signals the end of one cycle of yugas, an end-time after which the entire cycle will repeat itself.

3. THE EAGLE AND THE DOVE

1. It is important to draw a distinction between Kalki Krishnamurthy's own views and the customs that were held as glorious by the people of a millennium ago. Kalki did consider sati an abhorrent practice, but it is unlikely Tirukkovalur Malayaman would have seen it the same way.

4. THE AYYANAAR TEMPLE

1. This is a reference to the Tamil month of Aippasi, which corresponds roughly to the mid-October to mid-November period. 'Thulam' is the word for balance (weighing scale) and the word 'Thulamaadam', which means 'Balance Month' is a reference to the fact that the duration of day and night are equal during the month of Aippasi.
2. The form of Shiva riding his bull Nandi.
3. 'Naaval' is the Tamil word for jamun, and Naaval Theevu is a translation of 'Jambudvipa'.
4. Devotees of the goddess Shakti.
5. An ear ornament worn by men, usually a heavy ring.
6. Tirumann translates literally into 'holy mud' or 'holy clay'. This is also the name for the symbol of Vishnu, a white U-shaped or Y-shaped mark with a red line in the centre, like a trishul, that Vaishnavites draw on their foreheads, arms and shoulders.

8. TWO HANDS IN THE DARK

1. Karmic belief refers to good deeds as 'punyam' and bad deeds as 'paavam'. One is liberated from rebirth when the two have cancelled each other out, so it doesn't particularly pay to be too good or too bad.

9. THE BARKING DOG

1. The son of King Virata and brother of Princess Uttara, who served as Arjuna's charioteer when his own kingdom was attacked; he is known for his valour in the Kurukshetra war.

10. MANHUNT

1. 'Ejamaani' could mean 'employer, owner, boss or mistress'.

11. FRIEND? OR FOE?

1. 'Komagan' means 'son of the king'. It could also mean 'son of God', since the word 'ko' was used both for gods and kings, in line with the notion that the king was a divine representative on Earth.

14. WILL THE DREAM COME TRUE?

1. Kannan is the Tamil name for Krishna.

15. ROYAL RECEPTION

1. The bad luck believed to be brought by Saturn, known as 'Shani'.
2. 'Paatti' is Tamil for 'grandmother'. Aditya Karikalan refers to Nandini as the 'young grandmother of Pazhuvoor'.

16. OF MALAYAMAN'S ANXIETIES

1. A traditional folk art, where a bow is used as a musical instrument.
2. A word for 'grandfather', although the more common one is 'thatha'.

3. 'Kizhavar' is a slightly derogatory term for an old person. I have used the original Tamil term here because Aditya Karikalan will go on to refer to many of the conspirators by this term during his stay.

20. THE PHYSICIAN'S SON AGAIN

1. When Damayanti went in search of Nala, who had slipped away from her while they were sleeping in the forest, so that he would bring no more misfortune upon her, she was caught by a python. A hunter rescued her, but then tried to force himself on her. Damayanti's chastity apparently gave her the superpower of being able to burn someone on sight and she turned the hunter into a pile of ashes.
2. Poonguzhali's father is referred to by his caste here.

22. ANIRUDDHAR, BETRAYED

1. The act of clearing away the flowers and washing the vessels used for the morning prayer and decorating the altar with fresh flowers.

COMMOTION IN KADAMBUR

1. Maaman is literally mother's brother or the husband of one's own—or one's father's—sister, but can also be used as a form of address to an older man.

Also from ekadā

Also from ekadā

Also from ekadā